P9-DOB-057

HERO

Also by #1 Bestseller Mike Lupica:

Travel Team

Heat

Miracle on 49th Street

Summer Ball

The Big Field

Million-Dollar Throw

The Batboy

HERO

MIKE LUPICA

COCHRAN PUBLIC LIBRARY
174 BURKE STREET
STOCKBRIDGE, GA 30281

PHILOMEL BOOKS

An Imprint of Penguin Group (USA) Inc.

HENRY COUNTY LIBRARY SYSTEM
MCDONOUGH, STOCKBRIDGE, HAMPTON
LOCUST GROVE, FAIRVIEW

AN IMPRINT OF PENGUIN GROUP (USA) INC.

PHILOMEL BOOKS

A division of Penguin Young Readers Group.
Published by The Penguin Group. Penguin Group (USA) Inc., 375 Hudson Street, New York, NY 10014, U.S.A. Penguin Group (Canada), 90 Eglinton Avenue East, Suite 700, Toronto, Ontario M4P 2Y3, Canada (a division of Pearson Penguin Canada Inc.). Penguin Books Ltd, 80 Strand, London WC2R 0RL, England. Penguin Ireland, 25 St. Stephen's Green, Dublin 2, Ireland (a division of Penguin Books Ltd). Penguin Group (Australia), 250 Camberwell Road, Camberwell, Victoria 3124, Australia (a division of Pearson Australia Group Pty Ltd) Penguin Books India Pvt Ltd, 11 Community Centre, Panchsheel Park, New Delhi - 110 017, India. Penguin Group (NZ), 67 Apollo Drive, Rosedale, North Shore 0632, New Zealand (a division of Pearson New Zealand Ltd). Penguin Books (South Africa) (Pty) Ltd, 24 Sturdee Avenue, Rosebank, Johannesburg 2196, South Africa. Penguin Books Ltd, Registered Offices: 80 Strand, London WC2R 0RL, England.

Copyright © 2010 by Mike Lupica. All rights reserved. This book, or parts thereof, may not be reproduced in any form without permission in writing from the publisher, Philomel Books, a division of Penguin Young Readers Group, 345 Hudson Street, New York, NY 10014. Philomel Books, Reg. U.S. Pat. & Tm. Off. The scanning, uploading and distribution of this book via the Internet or via any other means without the permission of the publisher is illegal and punishable by law. Please purchase only authorized electronic editions, and do not participate in or encourage electronic piracy of copyrighted materials. Your support of the author's rights is appreciated. The publisher does not have any control over and does not assume any responsibility for author or third-party websites or their content.

Published simultaneously in Canada.
Printed in the United States of America.
Design by Richard Amari.
Text set in Candida.

Library of Congress Cataloging-in-Publication Data
Lupica, Mike. Hero / Mike Lupica. p. cm. Summary: Fourteen-year-old Zach learns he has the same special abilities as his father, who was the President's globe-trotting troubleshooter until "the Bads" killed him, and now Zach must decide whether to use his powers in the same way at the risk of his own life. [1. Heroes—Fiction. 2. Fathers and sons—Fiction. 3. Politics, Practical—Fiction. 4. Death—Fiction. 5. Family life—New York (State)—New York—Fiction. 6. New York (N.Y.)—Fiction.] I. Title. PZ7.L97914Her 2010 [Fic]—dc22
2010001772
ISBN 978-0-399-25283-9
1 3 5 7 9 10 8 6 4 2

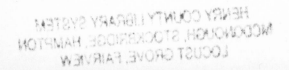

This one is for Michael Green.

I could never have written this book—or any
book—without the love and support of Taylor,
Christopher, Alex, Zach and Hannah.

They are my heroes, the ones who make
me believe in magic.

And Esther Newberg, who always just believes.

HERO

THERE were four thugs, total gangsters, in front of the house with their rifles and their night-vision goggles. Four more in back. No telling how many more inside.

So figure a dozen hard guys at least, protecting one of the worst guys in the world.

Not one of them having a clue about how much trouble they were really in, how badly *I* had *them* outnumbered.

Hired guns, in any country, never worried me. The Bads? They were the real enemy, worse than any terrorists, even if I was one of the few people alive who knew they existed.

Even my boss, the president of the United States,

didn't know what we were really up against, how much he really needed me.

When he talked about our country fighting an "unseen" threat, he didn't know how true that really was.

When my son, Zach, was little, I used to tell him these fantastic bedtime stories about the Bads, and he thought I was making them up. I wasn't.

The snow was falling hard now, bringing night along with it. Not good. Definitely not good. I didn't need a blizzard tonight, not if I wanted to get the plane in the air once I got back to the small terminal near the airport in Zagreb. Which was only going to happen if I could get past the guards, get inside, and then back out with the guy I'd come all this way for. It meant things going the way they were supposed to, which didn't always happen in my line of work.

My official line of work? That would be special adviser to the president. A title that meant nothing on nights like this. On assignments like this. The real job description was fixing things, things that other people couldn't, saving people who needed saving, capturing people who needed to be stopped. Dispensing my own brand of justice.

Sometimes I had help, people watching my back.

Not tonight. Tonight I was on my own. Not even the

president knew I was here. Sometimes you have to play by your own rules.

On this remote hill in northern Bosnia, near where the concentration camps had been discovered a few years before, I had managed to finally locate a Serb war criminal and part-time terrorist named Vladimir Radovic. He was known to governments around the world and decent people everywhere as Vlad the Bad because of all the innocent people he'd slaughtered when he was in power, before he was on the run.

To me, he was known by a code name, which I thought fit him much better:

The Rat.

I was here to catch the Rat.

Me, Tom Harriman. About to blow past the guns and inside a cabin that had been turned into an armed fortress.

Almost time now. I didn't just feel the darkness all around me, as if night had fallen out of the sky all at once. I could feel another darkness coming up inside me, the way it always did in moments like this, when something was about to happen. When I didn't have to keep my own bad self under control. When I could be one of the good guys but not have to behave like one.

The me that still scares me.

Time to go in and tell the Rat his ride was here.

I should have been cold, as long as I'd been waiting outside. And I knew I should be worried about what might go wrong. Only I wasn't. Cold *or* worried, take your pick.

As I moved along the front of the tree line, seeing the smoke coming out of the chimney, seeing both levels of the house lit up, I did wonder if it had been too easy finding him. Wondered if the Bads had *wanted* me to find him, as a way of drawing me here, making me vulnerable.

But that was always part of the fun of it, wasn't it? The finding out.

Someday when Zach is ready, when it is Zach's time and not mine, I will have to tell him the truth about the Bads and about me, tell my kid that the most fantastic story of all *was* me.

But for now it was time to be the unknown hero again, with the jeep waiting for me on the access road, over on the other side of the woods, with the jet waiting a few miles away in Zagreb. This wasn't the Tom Harriman who testified in front of Congress and briefed the intelligence agencies.

This was the Tom Harriman who did whatever it took to get the job done.

I began to move toward the left side of the house, my

boots not making a sound, even on the frozen snow. One of my many talents, gliding like I was riding an invisible wave.

The front four men were fanned out about fifty yards from the cabin, carrying their rifles like they were looking for any excuse to use them. They didn't know what I knew, that even if they *did* get to use them, the guns wouldn't do them much good.

And just like that I changed the plan, called an audible on myself, came walking out of the woods, in plain sight, talking to them in their native language.

"I'm lost," I said. "Can you help me out?"

Every gun turned toward me as the guards shouted at me to stop. But I just kept smiling, moving toward them, asking how to find my way back to the main road. I was such a stupid, they probably never met such a stupid in their lives.

The guy in charge just shook his head, turned and said something I couldn't hear, and they laughed, all of them dropping their guns at the same time, like a fighter dropping his hands.

I was on them before they knew it.

It was as if I'd covered the ground between us in one step. Another of my talents. Michael Jordan or LeBron never had a first step like this.

I put all four of them down before any of them could

get his gun back up. Wondered if they could hear the roar inside my head, the one I always heard. It was never adrenaline in times like this, it was something more, something I'd never been able to understand. Or control very well once the bell rang. Most people only see it happen in action movies, one against four, one guy using only his hands and feet for spins and kicks and jumps. Only this was no movie.

It was over quickly, the four of them laid out in the snow, arms splayed like snow angels. Done like dinner, as Zach would say.

It was then that I heard the crackle of the walkie-talkie from inside one of the guards' parkas. Heard a voice full of static, asking Toni why he wouldn't respond, that if he didn't respond right now, he was going to come looking for him.

I didn't know whether the voice was coming from behind the house, one of the four back there that I'd seen earlier, or from someone inside with the Rat.

Someone on the roof trained a huge searchlight on the front yard, making night as bright as day. The first shot was fired then, from somewhere off to my left. Then another. I ducked and rolled and went in a low crouch in the direction of the front door. They were probably wondering how I could still be moving like this, how they'd possibly missed me from close range.

I didn't have time to tell them they probably hadn't missed, that if they were going to put me down, they simply needed bigger guns.

They weren't putting me down and they weren't stopping me. I'd come too far to get the Rat, to take him to the people waiting for him in London, the ones who wanted to either hang him or put him away for the next ten thousand years.

I made it to the porch, the gunfire still crackling all around me.

First floor or second?

He was on the second floor. Don't ask me how I knew; I just did. Call it a sixth sense. So instead of crashing through the door, I jumped up to the second-floor landing.

Don't ask about making a jump like that. You either can or you can't.

I smashed the window and burst through. There he was, the fat slob, trying to make it to the door, turning to fire a shot with the gun in his right hand. But I was across the room before he could do anything, slapping the gun out of his hand, putting my hand behind his neck, finding the spot, putting him out.

I dragged him the rest of the way through the doorway, the two of us in the second-floor hallway. Here came two more of his guys, coming up the stairs with their guns raised but afraid to take the shot because I had pulled the Rat up in front of me, like one of those Kevlar vests you see on the cop shows. I wondered if the vests ever smelled as bad as he did.

It was the stink guys got on them when they were caught.

"Boys," I said to the guys on the stairs, "I'd love to stay and chat, but we've got a plane to catch. And I don't have to tell you what security is like at the airport these days."

"You're not going anywhere," the first one said.

"Well, yeah, actually I am," I said, and kicked him and his friend down the stairs. Then I was over them, flying toward the front door.

I had the Rat under my arm now. I'd played lacrosse in high school, had heard a story once about Jim Brown, who ended up becoming the greatest running back in pro-football history. Brown had been a lacrosse star himself in high school and later at Syracuse. He was so much bigger, stronger and faster than everyone else that he'd just pin his stick and the ball to his body, run down the field and score, again and again.

They'd had to change the rules so guys like him couldn't do that.

I pinned the Rat to me like that now, backing away from the house as more guys with guns appeared from every angle, all of them afraid to shoot because they might put one in the boss.

I thought about dropping him in the snow so I could go back and finish them all off, because when I got going like this, sometimes I couldn't stop myself.

But we really did have a plane to catch.

So I turned and ran into the woods, not worrying about the hidden trees or branches. I could see in the dark, even without those fancy night-vision goggles the Rat's boys had been wearing. Even with the hard snow pelting my face.

When I got to the other side of the woods, I looked down to the lights of the jeep, making sure that no one was waiting for me there.

It was just when you thought the hard part was over that the real danger began.

Nothing.

I threw the Rat in the backseat and peeled away, hearing the sound of cars starting up behind me. I tore off down the road toward Zagreb, taking the first turn like it was NASCAR.

My ride out of here, a Hawker 4000, was waiting on the runway, which was already covered in snow. I had told the kid who helped run the little terminal for his father that I worked for *his* president. I didn't tell him why I was here, just told him enough to pull him into tonight's action movie, like the two of us were playing Bond or Bourne.

I'd overpaid the kid by a *lot* for fuel and maintenance and told him what time I thought I'd be back and told him to have the wings de-iced. If not, the whole mission was a waste of time. Doomed to fail.

His eyes grew wide as plates when he counted the money. Then he nodded and promised me he'd do whatever I needed him to do. I told him that when the plane was in the air to take the money and the jeep he'd loaned me and keep driving until daylight because if he didn't, the guys I'd gone after would be going after him.

I saw two sets of headlights now. They looked to be a couple of minutes behind me, maybe less.

I pulled the jeep up to the plane, untied the Rat, dragged him out of the backseat.

"Him?" the kid said. "It was *him* you were after?" He crossed himself. Twice.

"Yeah," I said.

"He killed two of my uncles," the kid said. "In the war. Can't you just kill him here and let me watch?"

"Not my brand," I said. "Sorry."

Brand.

Another of Zach's expressions.

The Rat started to wake up. *Must be losing my touch,* I thought. Usually the claw was good for a few hours.

This time I just slapped him hard, twice, and back out he went.

Headlights from the first jeep appeared at the far end of the runway as I got behind the controls and started taxiing away from them. Soon enough the other jeep came barreling behind.

It was then, in the lights of the Hawker, that I saw a figure walking onto the runway. A man. He wasn't trying to stop me, wasn't carrying a weapon. Wasn't doing anything except standing in the lights, like all he wanted was for me to see him, hair as white as the falling snow showing underneath the old cap he wore down low over his eyes.

What are you doing here? I wondered.

You're supposed to be on the other side of the world. Not here.

I didn't have time to find out. The plane was already bumping down the runway, shimmying on the ice and snow. And we were airborne, the Rat and me, through the first level of clouds.

Gone.

I tried to focus on flying the plane, getting above the weather, flying until I had to refuel, as I knew I'd have to, between here and London.

But in my mind I kept seeing him on the runway, just standing there.

And that was the problem.

It was never what you thought, never *who* you thought.

I wanted to feel the rush you felt after you'd won, that feeling the great guys in sports told you they never got tired of. I should have felt *great*, really, bringing down the Rat, delivering him to people who'd been chasing him a lot longer than I had.

So why did I feel as if I were the one being chased? Even up here, all alone in the night sky?

ZACH Harriman needed to get home.

Not take his time crossing Central Park the way he usually did. Not stop at his favorite bench and read a book the way he sometimes did. Not try to kill a little more time before his dad came home.

Now.

He hadn't slept much the night before. He'd been feeling anxious. He always got this way before his dad came home from one of his "business trips."

Only Zach didn't think of them as regulation business trips. No one did. His dad worked for the government—worked for the *president,* actually—and Zach would often see him described as a "troubleshooting diplomat" in the newspapers or when he was being introduced on one of the TV news shows.

Zach didn't quite know what his dad did on these trips, but he had a feeling his dad was saving the world one bad place at a time. One time Zach had asked him what it was like, working for the president, and his dad had said in a quiet voice, "I work for the good guys."

He had gone off to Europe this time, some top-secret location Zach and his mom weren't allowed to know.

"That darned national security thing again," his dad had said, almost trying to make a joke of the danger he was probably going to be in.

But it was never a joke to Zach.

People—adults mostly, but kids at school, too—seemed to think every day was like some kind of holiday if you had a famous father. And Zach had to admit, no way around it, that it *was* a pretty cool deal, being Thomas Harriman's only child.

Except, it was way more cool when he was actually *around.*

A few months ago, his dad had been in Africa, and the news reports had showed him celebrating with some people he had led back across the border from South Africa into Zimbabwe. At the time, a commentator on CNN had said, "When this country needed him, there he was. Maybe Tom Harriman's real job is hero. And he goes wherever that job takes him."

But, see, that was it right there. That was the problem, to Zach's way of thinking.

The job *kept* taking his dad. He seemed to belong to the world.

And when you were fourteen, as Zach had just turned, the world that mattered the most to you was your own. Zach Harriman's world was his dad and his mom. It was Alba, Zach's nanny when he was younger, the family's housekeeper and cook now. And it was Kate, the fabulous Kate, Alba's daughter, because she and her mom lived with the Harrimans in their amazing apartment on Fifth Avenue—the top three floors of the great old brownstone Zach's eyes were fixed on now as he crossed the park.

Any kid wanted to have a dad who was brave and respected and famous, no doubt. And a hero, throw that in, too. Yet more than anything, Zach just wanted his dad to be home.

And he would be home tonight, flying his own plane as usual, landing it at Teterboro Airport over in New Jersey. Then he'd head back to the city by car.

Back home, Zach thought.

So Zach should have been happy. Like over-the-moon

happy, not a care in the world. He should have been killing time the way he usually did, because it was still only five o'clock and his dad wasn't scheduled to walk through the front door until seven at the earliest.

Only Zach *wasn't* happy. He was in a hurry, and a big one.

Starting to run.

And the thing was, he never rushed through the park unless he got caught in some kind of storm and had to beat it home. Other people might think of Central Park, built right in the middle of Manhattan, and think of the trees and green grass, the tennis courts, summer concerts, softball fields, skating rink, more water than most people knew about. And the zoo. And Zach was cool with all that.

But for Zach, Central Park was his own backyard.

The park was a place where he could be alone and not *feel* alone, where he could run the reservoir or kick a soccer ball around or just wander aimlessly and never be bored. Or stop and watch kids play touch football and pretend that he was in the game with them, that he was just a regular kid.

Sometimes he would walk over to the West Side after school—by himself—and spend an hour at the Museum of Natural History. Go hang with the dinosaurs who used to roam the earth the way his dad did now.

But not today.

Today he was running.

Running like he was being chased. Scared of something without knowing what.

Running hard.

He was close to Fifth Avenue now, could see he was going to make the light, didn't slow down as he crossed the avenue, nearly clipping a nanny he recognized from the neighborhood who was pushing a baby stroller.

He waved and yelled, "Sorry, Veronique!"

Then he slowed down just a little, like his dad downshifting one of his sports cars, as Lenny the doorman opened the front door for him.

"We need to talk about those Knicks," Lenny said.

"Later!" Zach said.

He took a hard right in the lobby, nearly skidding into the wall, heading for the elevator, the one that opened right up into the first floor of the apartment. Knowing the elevator would be waiting for him.

It was.

He took one last look over his shoulder, feeling totally whacked doing it, because he realized what he was doing. Looking to see if the Bads were gaining on him.

The elevator dinged and groaned and began to rise. Zach felt his stomach flip, as though the short ride up was a roller coaster.

The doors opened. Zach walked into the apartment, rounded the corner to the living room. Stopped dead in his tracks.

And he knew.

He knew before he saw all of them. Everyone staring at him with big eyes.

Sad eyes.

The saddest of all belonging to his mom, who clearly had been crying. His mom, who never even wanted anyone to see her crying at the movies.

The whole family was there. Alba. Kate. And John Marshall, the family lawyer, Uncle John to Zach his whole life, even though they weren't actually related.

With them were two policemen, staring at Zach along with everybody else.

Right there and then, Zach knew his dad wasn't coming home tonight. Wasn't coming home, ever.

He'd had it wrong, as it turned out.

The Bads hadn't been chasing him across Central Park after all.

They had been waiting for him here.

ZACH couldn't sleep that night.

He was cried out by the time he went to bed. Hugged out. *Worn* out.

But no matter how hard he tried, he couldn't sleep. He was alone now. No one to tell him he was going to get through this, over time. He knew the truth. That even when he did get to sleep, even when it was tomorrow, nothing was going to change. Nothing was going to make him feel better.

Nothing was going to bring back his dad.

Finally, a little past one in the morning, he slipped out of his room and quietly walked down the stairs, happy to see that all of the lights were out on the main floor of the apartment.

Zach opened the door to his dad's office, next to the den, where the two of them would watch games on the big-screen TV.

There was a huge desk in there, what had seemed to be the size of a battleship to Zach when he was younger. On the walls were photographs of his dad with famous politicians and other celebrities. One wall had nothing but photographs of the family. All of them smiling. All of them happy.

There was his dad's Harvard football jersey mounted in a glass case, a gift from Zach's mom.

The first varsity letter he'd gotten in football.

Two of the walls had floor-to-ceiling bookshelves built into them, with so many books Zach had always wondered how his dad fit them in here.

He could still smell his dad in here, feel him.

Could still hear his voice, his laugh, the jazz music he always had going when he was sitting behind the desk.

He remembered the last time the two of them had been in here together. It had turned into perhaps the most painful memory of all.

I barely had time for him.

Me, Zach thought. *The kid who was always complaining about my dad being away.*

And the last time I saw him?

I practically blew him off.

It had been a Thursday night. A school night, of course. But both Zach and Kate had two free periods to begin their Friday morning schedule, meaning neither one of them had a class until ten-thirty. So they'd hatched a plan at dinner to go to the movies.

No big deal at the time. There was no reason to feel as if he were ditching his dad because his dad wasn't supposed to be leaving for Europe until Saturday morning.

He'd poked his head into his dad's office to say goodbye. His dad was on the phone and he'd held up a finger to Zach. *I'll be just a moment.*

Zach checked his cell for the time.

"Piece of cake," his dad was saying.

The tone of his voice was pure Dad, the usual quiet cockiness Zach would hear when he talked business, even when Zach knew it was the president of the United States on the other end of the line.

"Yeah, yeah, yeah," Tom Harriman said, clearly wanting to wrap things up. But sounding hot at the same time. "No, you listen to me: sometimes the ones who tell you not to fight are the ones you should fear the most. The ones who say they want me to sit something out for my own good." Then he nodded and said, "Talk to you when I get back."

He placed the receiver in its cradle, calmer now, and said to Zach, "Hey, big boy. You off with Miss Kate?"

"She *really* wants to see this one. Swears it's funny."

"That's what your mother always tells me." Then his face turned serious. "Listen, I might have to take off earlier than I thought. They just sprang it on me."

Zach said, "Dad, you just got back. Now you gotta leave . . . when?"

"Dawn's early light. The boy with two frees to start the day will be sound asleep."

Zach didn't say anything. But his face must have told his dad everything. Tom Harriman said, "I know we haven't seen much of each other the past few months."

Before Zach could respond, they both heard Kate from upstairs calling Zach's name. The movie wasn't starting for another forty-five minutes and they were only a ten-minute walk from the theater, but Zach knew by now that Kate operated on her own timetable.

His dad said, "So I'm guessing the Knicks-Celtics game on TV tonight is out of the question?"

"Aw, Dad, you're killing me. But Kate *will* kill me if I bag on her now. So I'd better bounce."

"I get it," his dad said. "And you know why I get it? Because I'm a guy, that's why. We'll catch a real game at the Garden when I get back. *Many* games."

They were words that Zach'd heard plenty of times before from his dad. Maybe once too often.

"Yeah," he said to his dad, "sounds like a plan."

"Next time I'm back, I promise it won't seem like just another quick break from being gone again. Swear on our lucky coins."

Something else Zach had heard before.

"Okay," Zach said.

He could hear Kate in the foyer now, calling his name again. Time to go.

"You can wake me before you go if you want. I won't mind, promise."

"Wouldn't think about it," his dad answered. Zach started to move out the door, but his dad stopped him. "Hey, Zacman?"

"Yeah, Dad?"

"Be good."

"Always, Dad. Gotta roll now, though."

His dad was asleep when Zach got back from the movies. Gone when Zach woke up in the morning.

Gone for good.

IT had been a full month since his dad had died in the plane crash, nowhere near Teterboro Airport. Instead, the Learjet had gone down on the eastern end of Long Island, closer to the Harrimans' summer home in East Hampton than to Fifth Avenue.

Three weeks since the big funeral.

Two weeks since Zach had gone back to school.

Sometimes Zach could go a whole ten minutes without thinking about it.

Sometimes not.

Accepting it, that's what the grown-ups said he had to do. Even Kate said he had to find a way to deal with his dad's death and start moving on, which sort of figured, since Kate seemed to know more about things than most grown-ups Zach had met.

So he was: dealing with it, accepting it, coming to terms. All the different ways of saying it he got from the grief therapist his mom had sent him to see.

Abso*lutely*, he wanted to say to the woman, Dr. Abbott. *I think I've pretty much got it now. A month ago I'm strolling through the park, literally, with one life—one life and two parents—and now I've got another one.*

Life, that is.

Yeah, no worries, Doc.

The kid who'd wanted his dad to be home *more* now had one who wasn't coming home *ever.* The kid who just wanted to be regular was never going to be regular again. The kid who didn't want to feel so alone felt more alone than ever. Check, check, check.

Zach knew these were the things Dr. Abbott *wanted* to hear from him when she was telling him in her soft voice that it was all right for him to open up to her. But he never said any of them out loud, not in the six sessions with her he'd had in the two weeks before he went back to school. Because by the end of the second week, it was mission accomplished, at least in his mind. He'd convinced her—and his mom—that he was dealing and accepting and coming to terms enough that he didn't need to see her anymore, at least for now.

That was key, telling them that he'd go back to therapy on the dead run if he thought he needed to. But he had other needs at the moment.

"I gotta stop talking about this now" is the way he'd explained it to his mom.

"Not talking about it every day is one thing," she'd answered Zach. "But that doesn't mean you get to bottle things up."

"Mom," he'd said. "I pretty much emptied that bottle for Dr. Abbott. If I want to talk about Dad from now on, I'll do it with you. Or with Kate. Nothing against the doc, but the two of you are way smarter about me than she is."

His mom had smiled then. "Kate being the smarter of the two of us, of course."

"Didn't say that."

"Didn't have to."

She'd gone along, though. Then Zach was back in school, getting back into his normal routines, going to class, waiting for basketball to start, even throwing himself into doing his homework. Actually doing it early every day so he could get back on his computer for what he considered his real homework:

Finding out every single thing he could about his dad's plane crash.

Which Zach believed was no accident, no matter what

everyone said. There had been no evidence of terrorism or tampering. No distress call from his dad to air traffic control.

But no reason why the engines had just quit, either.

His dad would have figured something out, Zach was sure, if he'd had any kind of chance. . . .

So this was something else he hadn't said out loud to Dr. Abbott, or his mom, or Kate.

They'd all told him to stay busy, keep occupied. Okay. He kept himself busy reading up on the crash, on planes like his dad's, on other crashes like this one that nobody had ever explained.

When his mom would poke her head inside his door and ask him what he was working on so late, he'd say, "School project."

"What subject?"

"History," he'd say, and not feel as if he were lying.

Then he'd get up in the morning and he and Kate would make the twenty-minute walk up Fifth and then one block over to the Parker School. Once he was there, he would try to get through another day, even though it now felt like the Bads were with him all the time.

And the other kids at school weren't helping, even though Zach could see them trying. He had two other buds besides Kate at school, both of them kids from basketball. Josh Morris was his best friend on the team, and its biggest player. And Zach usually loved hanging around with Dave Epstein, the team's second-string point guard, because Dave was probably the funniest kid at Parker. Like *Family Guy* funny.

Zach loved playing ball with them, loved the fact that he was just good enough as an outside shooter and a defender to crack Parker's starting lineup. He was always happy to see the start of basketball season coming up on him and sorry in the spring to see it end.

But even Josh and Dave didn't know how to act around him now. They treated him like he was sick or something.

So now Zach felt like even more of an outsider at school. Even with people going out of their way to be nice to him.

Even Spencer Warren had stopped torturing him for the time being.

Zach knew in his heart that Spence—president of their class, captain of the football, basketball and baseball teams, pretty much the captain of the whole school—was putting on an act, trying to act as concerned as everybody else. Because up until the crash, Zach had always considered his relationship with Spence Warren give-and-take:

Spence gave grief and Zach took it.

Not the kind of grief his mom and Dr. Abbott were

worried about. No, this was the kind of grief that kids had given other kids at school since the beginning of recorded time.

Zach had never thought about it this way until now. But after being with Dr. Abbott, he was convinced that there really ought to be grief counselors for the kind Spence gave him.

And always for the same reason.

Kate.

Spence wanted Kate for himself, simple as that. He hated that Zach and Kate were so close. He hated how much time they spent together, took every opportunity to make Zach pay for it. He told Zach over and over that the only reason the prettiest and smartest girl at Parker paid any attention to him was because her mom worked for Zach's parents.

"Kate's mom may be the paid help at your house," Spence said to him one time, "but Kate is your paid help everywhere else."

Even though Spence was bigger and stronger than Zach by a lot, even knowing a fight would get them both suspended from Parker, Zach knew he shouldn't have let that one go. He should have thrown down right there, thrown a punch. Getting just one solid punch in would have been worth it.

Zach knew that if you took something like that and let

it go, then you were going to be taking it for as long as the two of you were in school together.

But he took it anyway. The way he always had.

Just said, "Yeah, good one, Spence, you got me again," and walked away. But not before he heard Spence say, "By the way, freak boy? I ever find out you're telling Kate about any of our conversations about her? You go to the top of my smack list."

Like Zach wasn't there already.

He just kept walking that day. One more time, one more threat from Spence burning in his ears, when he wondered how he could possibly be Tom Harriman's kid.

Tom Harriman: who wasn't afraid of anything or anybody, probably not even at the very end . . .

But there Spence had been Zach's first day back, all these other kids around, Kate included, putting out his hand and saying, "Just speaking for the class, sorry about your dad, dude. We all are."

Zach'd had no choice but to shake the outreached hand. As he did, Spence had said, "I don't know what else to say."

"Then don't," Zach had wanted to say.

But he said nothing, as usual.

Since then, the only times Spence had gone out of his way to say anything nice, act like an actual human being, were when Kate was around. Other than that, he'd pretty much left Zach alone. Not such a bad thing. Maybe even the one *good* thing that had come out of this whole experience, getting Spence out of his face.

So why exactly was he standing next to Zach's locker now, when school had been out for an hour?

ZACH had been in the library, getting the jump on his homework, waiting for Kate to finish with play rehearsal.

Kate played sports—soccer in the fall and lacrosse in the spring. But what she really loved to do was sing. She had what Zach's mom always described as a Broadway voice. In the fall, it seemed like she always had one of the starring roles in Parker's annual musical. This year's show was *High School Musical*.

Zach had told her that it was just as easy for him to do homework in school, and that he'd wait for her so they could walk home together.

Only now Spence was the one waiting for *him*, saying, "What're you doing here so late, Harriman?"

Just the two of them now. No handshakes when Zach

got to his locker, no fake concern. No need for Spence
Warren to do the kind of acting job that Kate was doing
upstairs in the Performing Arts Center.

Lie or tell the truth?

Truth, he decided. It was a way for him, at least inside, to feel like less of a wimp. Like he was standing
up to Spence. "Meeting Kate here in a few minutes," he
said.

Spence nodded.

"Right," he said.

"Play practice," Zach said.

Spence said, "So you two can walk home together."
Not a question, just a statement of fact. Spence nodded
again.

"Yeah," Zach said, opening his locker door, trying to
find a place for his books in the mess in there. Hoping
the conversation was over.

Knowing it wasn't.

Knowing the old Spence was back.

"Must be tough," Spence said. "Being you right now.
Your dad and all."

Everybody else at school had at least stopped talking
about it.

Zach kept himself busy, rearranging his locker. "Gets
a little easier every day," he said. "You know."

"Man, I don't see how that could be," Spence said.

He leaned against the locker next to Zach's, Dave Epstein's, as if settling in for a while. "Seriously, dude? How can that be possible? I mean, if it were me? My dad dying like that? I don't think I could ever get over it."

Don't let him get to you, Zach told himself. Feeling like some kind of red warning sign was flashing inside his head. *Walk away.* But he was stuck here, knowing he couldn't tell Spence he had to be someplace, had already told him this was where he was supposed to be, waiting for Kate.

Leaving would just be another way of running away.

"Oh, it's like grown-ups are always telling you," Zach said, keeping his tone casual, not wanting to give Spence the satisfaction of knowing he was getting to him. "What doesn't kill you makes you stronger."

"But, see, that's what I'm trying to say," Spence said. "This must be killing you even worse than it would somebody else."

Zach blew out some air, feeling tired all of a sudden. "Why is that?"

"Well, if it was *me*, at least I'd have a lot of friends at school, having my back, so to speak. But let's face it, you being you, all you've pretty much got is Kate."

Behind that came a grin that Zach knew as well as he knew the way to school, the look of total triumph.

Why wouldn't he feel that way? Spence Warren was starting a fight with Zach he never lost.

"And Kate pretty much *has* to take care of you, right?"

It always came back to her.

The words just came out of Zach now, before he had a chance to stop them.

"Shut up, Spence."

If he wasn't standing up to him exactly, at least he wasn't backing down.

Spence looked confused now, as if Zach had said something to him in a foreign language. *"Shut up?"* he said. "Dude, I thought we were just conversing here."

"No," Zach said. Not just feeling tired now, feeling exhausted. "No, we weren't. You just waited for the right time to start busting my *stinking* chops again. Now *that* must have killed *you,* having to wait a whole month to start up again. Did you have to go find somebody else to practice on while I was away?"

Spence still hadn't moved, was still leaning against Dave's locker, looking so relaxed he could fall asleep right there.

And in that moment, Zach saw himself slapping that self-satisfied look off his face, slapping him hard, then grabbing him by the front of his gray Parker hoodie and

banging him hard into Dave's locker, imagining the surprise on his face, the shock, even the pain . . .

A Zach he didn't know.

Spence said, "I'm sorry, what did you say, Harriman?
I stopped listening after *shut up.*"

"Too bad, you missed some really good conversing."

"You did tell me to shut up, didn't you?"

"It's a shame Kate's not here, Spence," Zach said. "So
she could see just how much of a loser you really are."

Now Spence straightened up. Not grinning any longer. "You're calling me names now?"

"Yeah," Zach said. "I guess I am."

Spence dropped the books he'd been carrying, got
right up on Zach, slamming his locker door closed as he
did, the sound echoing up and down the empty hall.

"You're gonna need to take that back."

"Take it back?" Zach shook his head. He felt himself
grinning now. "What are you, seven years old? No kidding, Spence, for a smart guy you can sound dumber
than a bag of hammers."

One of his dad's old expressions popping into his
head, out of nowhere.

Where did *that* come from? Where was *all* of this coming from?

In a quiet voice, Spence said, "So let me get this

straight: Now I'm *dumb* on top of everything else?" Zach could feel the heat of Spence's breath on his face, like exhaust.

Spence wasn't all that much taller than Zach. He'd just always seemed taller; Zach felt as if he'd been looking up at the guy as long as he'd known him. Like having Spence in his life had given him a permanent stiff neck.

"Stop it! Both of you! Stop it right now!"

Kate.

Zach and Spence both turned. There she was at the end of the row of lockers, hands on hips. Like a teacher.

Spence spoke first, smiling at her. His class president smile. "Stop what?"

Kate said, "How about whatever's going on here? How would that be?"

"Nothing interesting going on here," Spence said. "Right, Harriman?"

There was no point in getting Kate in the middle of this, even though she was always in the middle, right there between him and Spence, whether she was actually around or not.

"We were just messing around," Zach said. "You think I'd actually pick a fight with *this* guy?"

"Right," Kate said. Knowing both of them were lying,

and not liking it from Zach. She looked at him carefully, then decided to let it go.

"You ready to roll?" she said.

"Yeah."

To Spence she said, "See *you* tomorrow, Mr. Warren."

"Done deal," Spence said.

Just like that he picked up his books and was gone, around the corner, up some stairs.

Kate said, "Do I want to know?"

Zach said, "No."

Then she looked down at her own books and said, "Idiot!"

"*Okay,*" Zach said. "I'm sorry."

"I mean *me,*" she said. "I left my jacket in the auditorium."

"Total idiot, you're right."

"Shut up," she said, smiling at him for the first time. "Meet you on the bricks in five."

Outside.

"Yes, ma'am."

"Don't 'ma'am' me," she said. "I'm not your mother."

As she walked away, he said, "Act like you are sometimes."

Without looking back, she said, "Heard that."

He watched her disappear up some steps and realized he hadn't exactly been glad she'd shown up when she had.

It was then that Zach felt something and looked down.

Looked down and saw something he'd never seen before, no matter how angry he'd gotten at Spence, no matter how badly he'd been humiliated:

Clenched fists.

His hands and his arms shaking, because that's how hard he wanted to hit something. Practically his whole body shaking. Not with fear this time.

With something else.

Without thinking about what he was doing, or where he was going, he walked slowly down the row of lockers to one of the old brick walls at the basement level of Parker, one with old photographs on it, from sports teams out of the past.

He found an empty place in the wall and just like that started pounding his fists into it. First a right, then a left, and then no pattern—just all these wild, random punches. Zach threw them with everything he had.

The punches he'd imagined himself throwing at Spence Warren when he was still there in front of him.

When he was finally done, out of breath and dripping with sweat the way he had been when he ran home across the park the day his dad died, he looked down again, expecting to see his fists bruised, his knuckles raw and covered with blood.

Zach saw nothing.

More amazing, considering the fact that he'd just gone twelve rounds with a brick wall?

He *felt* nothing.

ZACH wasn't the only one trying to settle back into the old routines and fit them around his new life.

His mom was, too.

Even before his dad had died, his mom had been working hard to help get Senator Robert Kerrigan of New York elected president, and not just because Senator Kerrigan went all the way back to Harvard with Zach's dad the way Uncle John did. She believed in the good of the man. It was why she was back into the campaign full-time, throwing herself into it harder than ever.

His mom, Elizabeth Townsend Harriman, was pretty famous herself. She was the daughter of a former U.S. senator, niece of a former secretary of state, and now ran the Townsend Foundation, traveling the world to give Townsend Foundation money away to people in need.

"I need the work," she had explained to Zach, "I need the outlet, I need something to take my mind off what happened. And on top of all that? This country needs Bob Kerrigan."

"Mom," Zach said. "You don't have to explain to me. I know how much Dad liked Senator Kerrigan. I see him sometimes on TV, and even I like listening to his speeches."

Senator Kerrigan had been a few years behind Zach's dad at Harvard. And both of them had ended up in government service. Tom Harriman had become President Addison's troubleshooter, the globe-trotter. Bob Kerrigan had started out as a New York City lawyer, become a judge and gone to work in the Justice Department before finally becoming President Addison's attorney general.

But eventually he'd moved back to New York and run for the U.S. Senate and won. Last year he'd surprised everybody—including Zach's mom and dad—by announcing in the middle of his first term in the Senate that he was going to run to succeed President Addison, whose term limit of eight years was almost up.

And he was supposed to be the same kind of long shot, the same kind of inexperienced guy that Zach knew

President Addison had been. Except now he was the front-runner in the polls, even running against the current vice president, Dick Boras. Zach's mom had explained to him that usually the sitting vice president was a shoo-in to get the nomination.

Just not this time.

When Zach had asked why not, she'd said, "Because Vice President Boras is old and mean and Bill Addison never should have picked him as a running mate in the first place."

"Works for me," Zach'd said.

Tonight, his mom was holding a fund-raiser for Senator Kerrigan at their apartment, her first big social occasion of any kind since Zach's dad had died. Down the road, there would be a much bigger New York City event for Senator Kerrigan in Central Park, one that Zach's mom was already planning in her head. For now, she was using the Harriman name—and Townsend, her maiden name—to attract people who were willing to make contributions to the Kerrigan campaign.

"Small crowd," she said, "but deep pockets."

"Ooh," Zach said, "rich people. My *favorite!*"

"Hush," his mom said, "and go make sure your nice clothes are clean."

He used an old line of his dad's on her then, knowing it would make her smile.

"Don't worry about me tonight, Mom," he said. "I promise not to bother the decent people."

She pointed upstairs. "Go," she said. "I have to go into the kitchen now and yell at the caterer a little more."

But she looked happy just to be busy, the first time she had really looked that way to Zach since the funeral. That was good enough for him.

He was keeping himself busy, too, on a campaign of his own.

Just not one that he wanted to tell anybody about yet.

Zach put on the same blazer and tie he'd worn to his dad's funeral, telling himself that they were just clothes, that putting them on didn't mean you had to be sad all over again.

Kate was in the new dress Alba had bought for her.

"You look great," Zach said when she came to his room to get him.

"And you," Kate said, "you look about as happy to be dressed up as you always are." And then she couldn't help herself and straightened his tie.

Zach had never seen a politician give a speech in person. He had met plenty of them, gotten to shake Senator Kerrigan's hand at the funeral, and even President Addison's. But he had never been in a crowd like the one in his living room, some people sitting, most standing, Secret Service guys with their dark suits and earpieces leaning against walls, standing in front of windows, taking in the whole scene.

But as soon as Senator Kerrigan started talking, Zach understood why everyone had come to hear him and meet him.

And give him boatloads of money.

"*I* would have paid to see this," Kate said in a whisper from where they were standing, near a door to the kitchen. Zach had promised his mom that they'd stay out of the way for the most part.

"Same," Zach said.

"He's talking to some of the biggest and most famous people in New York," Kate said, "but it's like he could be talking to our class."

Senator Kerrigan began by talking specific issues, about war and immigration and the economy. But then he shifted to the difference in life between talking tough and actually being tough, about courage and honor and doing the right thing and trusting your instincts and never wavering on your core beliefs. It was all in the context of talking about America, but somehow Zach felt as if the senator were talking directly to *him*.

And Zach knew everybody in the apartment, including Kate, felt exactly the same way.

Eventually Senator Kerrigan talked about Zach's dad, how nobody forced him to serve his country, how he wasn't drafted into doing so. How he'd decided on his own that service, courage and honor were his destiny.

"Tom Harriman was smart enough to know that a person can never escape his or her identity," Senator Kerrigan said. "You can try to ignore it, but you can't hide from it. Tom Harriman hid from no one."

The room burst into applause, Zach clapping harder than anybody, feeling the tears in his eyes.

Senator Kerrigan wasn't finished. "Tom Harriman was the finest man I've met," he said. "He's the one who convinced me that I was the right person to succeed Bill Addison. So here I am, trying to do that, asking for your support." He grinned. "And trying to empty your pockets."

When the laughter died down, he was serious again. "It is time for all of us to embrace the destiny, the true mission for the United States of America, in good times and bad. We must all be strong; we must all be brave." His voice rising now, as if the windows were open and he wanted the whole city to hear him. "We must honor this country's ideals in the same way I honor the memory of the man who lived in this home where we have come together tonight."

The room exploded with applause again. Even the

ones who had been sitting on couches and chairs jumped to their feet. Zach looked across at his mom, who seemed to be smiling and crying at the same time, applauding along with everybody else.

"Wow," Kate said. "Wow wow wow."

Zach said, "I want to start campaigning for him tonight."

"Take me with you," she said.

They went upstairs then, Kate to finish her homework, Zach to get back on his laptop. About an hour later he heard a surge in the conversation level, walked briefly out of his room, looked downstairs and saw people starting to leave.

A few minutes later there was a knock on his door. When he opened it, Senator Kerrigan was standing there. He had taken off his tie by then, unbuttoned the jacket to his suit. It occurred to Zach that the senator reminded him a little bit of George Clooney, but with even grayer hair.

"Awesome speech," Zach said.

"You listened from up here?"

Zach said, "I was hiding in the back."

"They seemed to like it."

"Are you *joking*?" Zach said. "They loved it. Now I know why my mom is working so hard to get you the nomination."

Senator Kerrigan placed a hand on Zach's desk chair and said, "May I?" Zach nodded. The senator sat and Zach took a seat at the end of the bed.

"This probably won't come as a shock to you," Senator Kerrigan said, grinning. "But sometimes I feel as if I'm working for her."

Zach heard a buzzing sound. Senator Kerrigan whipped out his BlackBerry, nodded in a tired way.

"Listen, I've got to be going. I'm flying to Ohio tonight. But before I left, I wanted you to know how I felt about your dad. That wasn't just another campaign speech downstairs. That came from the heart. He really *was* the finest man I've ever known."

"Thanks," Zach said. "Me too."

The senator said, "The world became less safe as soon as he was gone. And our enemies probably see an opening."

Zach just sat there, listening to him now the way he had downstairs, still trying to process the fact that somebody who might be the next president of the United States was actually sitting in his room.

Senator Kerrigan stood up. So did Zach. The senator said, "We'll have a longer talk about this the next time we're together." He put out his hand and Zach shook it, hearing his dad's voice in his head as he did, making sure he looked Senator Kerrigan right in the eyes. "Your father was willing to do whatever it took to keep our enemies from winning. So am I."

"I believe you, sir," Zach said.

"Be strong," Senator Kerrigan said. "You be strong, Zach Harriman."

Then he turned and left.

Zach stood there in the middle of the room, feeling the man's presence even with him gone.

Then he quietly said what Kate had said earlier.

"Wow wow wow."

The loud voices from downstairs woke him up, his clock radio saying it was three minutes after midnight.

At first Zach thought he might have been dreaming, but then the voices got louder.

He got out of bed, pushed his door open a couple of inches, realized immediately that it was his mom and Uncle John. He had never once heard them argue about anything. But they sure seemed to be arguing about something now.

"John," Elizabeth Harriman said, "lower your voice."

"Just because I don't agree with you," he said, "doesn't mean I'm shouting."

"Well, it certainly sounds that way to me."

The two of them were standing in front of the elevator, Uncle John's coat over his arm.

"I'm right about this," he said. "Sometimes it seems as if you've joined a cult."

"I'm working for a candidate I believe in," she said. "One my husband—who was your best friend in the world—believed in just as passionately."

"Tom only saw the things in Bob Kerrigan he wanted to see," Uncle John said. "The same slick, polished Bob Kerrigan the voters are seeing."

"You're saying he's a phony?" she said.

Uncle John shook his head. "They're *all* phonies," he said. "He just happens to be the one who's trying to become president. He's neither prepared nor strong enough, despite all his fancy words about strength and toughness."

"Were you *watching* the audience tonight?" Zach's mom said. "Did you see how his message resonated with them?"

"They're in love with the *words*. Everybody is these days. But it takes more than words to lead this country."

Now Zach heard the anger in his mother's voice again, her voice rising even though she had just told Uncle John to keep his down. "It's not just rhetoric, John. It's ideas. And ideals. He's a man of great substance."

"He's a man of great style."

"You're wrong," she said. "I'm not sure I've ever

heard you be this wrong about anything. And you're not going to change my mind about him."

"It's the obligation of the family lawyer to do that," he said, "even when it's the head of the family who's wrong."

"You can do that the next time I am," she said. "Now good *night*."

Zach watched as she pressed the elevator button for him, turned and walked into the kitchen.

So she didn't see the look on Uncle John's face, the anger in it as he watched her go, an Uncle John even Zach didn't recognize.

Next to the elevator door, on a table for everyone who entered the apartment to see, was a framed photograph Zach's mom had placed there: Tom Harriman and Senator Kerrigan when they were much younger, the two of them standing on Pennsylvania Avenue with the White House behind them, arms around each other.

As the elevator door opened, Uncle John took the picture out of its stand, took a long look at it, one hand holding the door open.

Then he slammed it hard on the table and left.

BE strong," Senator Kerrigan had said to Zach.

It just made him more determined than ever to find out the truth behind his father's death.

He had yet to find anything he could classify as a clue, despite *weeks'* worth of reading. It was why he wasn't ready to bring Kate in on this yet, even knowing she could probably help. As good as Zach's brain was, hers was usually better.

Yet there was another reason he was keeping her in the dark: because he was afraid that when he did tell her, even if he had something, she was going to think this was the total exact opposite of moving on with his life.

So for now he'd just keep at it on his own. He'd bookmarked some stuff on the Web, printed out some of it and stuck it in the bottom drawer of his desk with old school papers, into a clutter he figured even one of those *CSI* units would have a hard time sorting out.

Zach Harriman was staying strong.

Zach's mom was out of town on a trip to help Senator Kerrigan. Zach, Kate and Alba had just finished dinner together.

Alba told them both to shoo, despite Zach's offer to help clear the table. "I don't need your help in my kitchen," she said. "Go."

And it *was* hers, Zach knew. Oh man, they all knew. Even Elizabeth Harriman acted like she had to get permission to go into the kitchen when Alba was cooking.

Zach and Kate went to the second-floor den and turned on the Knicks game. Kate didn't care about basketball, but she'd started watching the games at night just to keep Zach company, knowing that when his dad was around—when his dad was still alive—watching the Knicks was something Zach had done with him.

Tonight, though, he sensed that she wasn't just there to keep him company; she had something else on her mind. She was paying even less attention to the game than usual.

Which was saying something.

"Okay," she finally said from her end of the couch. "I've got a fun game we can play. How about we each tell the other the secret we've been keeping!"

This was not good, he knew right away. *Definitely* not good. He could tell by the tone of her voice, the fake excitement in it.

Zach's immediate response was to just stare at the Knick on the foul line as if he were about to take the most important free throw in the history of the NBA.

"Should I go first?" she said. "Or do you want to?"

Zach said, "Why don't we just *watch* the game instead of playing one?"

"Okay, if that's the way you want it," she said, ignoring him, folding her legs underneath her as she turned to face him. "I'll go."

The Knick made the first free throw.

"Oh, wait," Kate said. "I *can't* go first. Want to know why?"

"Not a clue."

"*Because I haven't been keeping any secrets from you, that's why.*"

He turned his head. She was at least smiling at him. "Your turn," Kate said.

"I haven't been keeping any secrets from you, either," Zach said.

"Liar."

"I haven't."

"Yeah, you have," she said. "All the closed doors at night. You saying you're doing homework when I know better than anybody that you don't have it in you to sit that long for anything having to do with school."

"Since you know so much," Zach said, "why don't you tell me what it is? Then we'll both know."

"I've got a better idea," she said. "Why don't *you* come clean with *me* and save us both a lot of time. And you a lot of misery."

She was going to wear him down on this, Kate style, the way Spence could wear him down *about* her. If there was one thing about Kate that came closest to annoying him, it wasn't that she was so smart. It was that she could be so cocky about it.

She always thought she was right. And she wouldn't give up until you admitted it.

He tried to explain it to his dad one time and his dad had laughed and said, "She looks like a sweetie pie, but if Kate Paredes goes up for a rebound, she *is* coming down with the ball."

It was like that now, Zach Harriman knowing he was going to lose this battle sooner or later, deciding it might as well be sooner.

"Okay, I give up," he said.

"A wise decision," Kate said. "You're just one eighth

grader from the Parker School trying to stop my eventual plans for world domination."

He muted the TV set. The room was completely quiet now. There was just the blur of the action from the game.

"I've been reading up on my dad's crash," he said.

Kate said, "And why, more than a month after it happened, are you doing something like that?"

"Why?" he said. "Because I want to *know* what happened, that's why."

"You do know," she said. "Everybody does. The engines failed and your dad tried to land in the bay. He didn't make it and crashed into that field instead."

She held up a hand, letting him know she wasn't quite finished. "And I thought the whole goal right now was to put as much distance as possible between you and all that."

What did his dad used to say? Another one of his goofy expressions?

In for a dime, in for a dollar.

If he was going to tell Kate some of it, he might as well tell her all of it.

"I don't think it was an accident," he said.

"Wait a second," she said. "You're saying that you think somebody sabotaged your dad's airplane?"

"Yes."

"When he . . . when it happened, you said no way your dad would let a plane he was flying crash," Kate said.

Her eyes were on him hard, like a flashlight being shined on him in the darkened room.

"Right," Zach said. "And we agreed that no one *lets* an accident happen. It just happens." He put air quotes around *happens,* shrugged and said, "I was lying."

"To me," she said.

"Not just to you, to everybody," he said. "I didn't buy that it was an accident when it happened and I'm not buying it now. He was just too good a pilot. Like he was too good at everything else."

Except being around, of course.

Except being *here.*

"But it wasn't pilot failure," Kate said. "It was engine failure."

"That's what the investigators said. I know that's what they *think.* But they don't *know.* Because on top of everything else, they can't find the black box. And there's no record of him making a distress call to the airport in East Hampton, which was the closest one, or anywhere else."

Kate said the next part in a soft voice, like she was telling him that she didn't want to argue with him, or have a debate about this, or beat him up on it. "Planes crash all the time," she said, "all over the world. Some-times there's an official explanation, sometimes there isn't. Remember that paper I did on Amelia Earhart? Sometimes the plane just disappears."

Zach said, "Listen, even if something had gone terri-bly wrong and he knew that he couldn't pull out of it, he would have used his chute and bailed out. So why didn't he do that?"

"Maybe there wasn't time," she said. "Maybe he just never got the chance."

"But see, that's the thing!" he said. "My dad was at his best under pressure! The worst trouble always brought out the best in him. That's why there has to be a reason he didn't *get* the chance to save himself. And I'm going to find out why."

Neither one of them said anything now. Zach turned his head back toward the television, where somebody on Charlotte had just made this amazing dunk, throw-ing the ball down so hard Zach was surprised he and Kate couldn't hear it over the mute button.

"Don't do this," Kate said.

"I have to."

"You know I've got you no matter what you do," she said.

"I know," he said. "I *know*."

"But you've got to let this go," she said.

He shook his head slowly, side to side.

"Please listen to me," she said. "Listen, because I sometimes feel like I know you better than I know myself. And I know that if you *don't* let this go, you're going to get so lost in it that even I won't be able to find you."

"No."

"No to which part?"

"No, I'm not letting it go. And no, I could never get that lost; you'd invent a new kind of GPS if that's what it took for you to find me."

"You really and truly believe somebody killed your dad?"

"Yes."

"Let's say you're right," Kate said, "even though I'm not really saying that. Who would do something like that?"

"You want the short list, just from the last couple of years?" he said. "Or the longer one from his whole career?"

"And you really believe a fourteen-year-old can find something that nobody else has?" Kate said.

"Yeah," he said. "Yeah, I do."

ZACH tried to stay with the game after Kate was gone but knew he was going through the motions with the Knicks the way he was with a lot of things lately. Letting people think he was the same old Zach, when he was never going to be that Zach again.

Maybe things would be a little different when he was back *playing* basketball again instead of just watching it, when he was back on the court with the guys, getting a chance to channel his energy.

Only it wasn't just energy he needed to blow off. It was the anger he was carrying around with him, making him feel like some kind of ticking bomb.

All in all, he thought he did a pretty good job of keeping a lid on it, hiding it from everyone, even Kate. Maybe not doing such a bang-up job of hiding it when he tried to beat up the brick wall that day. But most of the time.

Problem was, he was mad *all* of the time. And as much as he needed to know everything he could about the crash, as sure as he was that somebody had sabotaged his dad, reading up on it only made him madder.

He knew he wasn't the only kid in the world something like this had happened to. He knew that really bad things happened all the time, and to good people. They got sick and died. They got hit by hurricanes in New Orleans. Earthquakes. Tsunamis.

9/11.

It didn't change what he felt, and what he felt was that he didn't just have a dark cloud following him around lately; it was as if the thunder and lightning were inside him.

Were him.

He was upstairs now, on the balcony outside his bedroom, staring out at the park. In his hand was the rare Morgan silver dollar, an 1879, his dad had given him once as a present, with Lady Liberty on it. He'd told Zach that even though it was made of silver, it was worth its weight in gold.

And something he should never lose.

"Why?" Zach had said.

"Are you chafing on me?" his dad had said, throwing one of Zach's expressions back at him. "Because I gave it to you, that's why. And because it's gonna be the only good luck charm you'll ever need."

Zach tried to squeeze some luck out of the Morgan now as he stared at the buildings on the other side of the park. The view was amazing as always, but it was doing nothing for him. He kept replaying the conversation with Kate inside his head, thinking of ways he could have made her understand better what he was doing and why he had to do it. Only here was the person who said she knew him better than anybody, and probably did, saying he was nuts to think that somebody had knocked his dad out of the sky video-game style.

He needed to go out.

Needed to do something more than turn on his computer, even though it was past nine o'clock. Needed to *move*. Needed not to be here. Zach walked back into his room, grabbed his Knicks hoodie off a hanger in his closet, hoping that Kate and Alba were in their rooms at the back end of the first floor, knowing Alba would never let him go out alone at this time of night if he asked her for permission.

But Zach wasn't asking.

All that dark stuff he was carrying around, maybe it belonged outside in the night.

He didn't push the elevator button, didn't want to take the chance Kate or Alba would hear it opening and closing. He went out the back door to the kitchen instead, willing to take the stairs all the way down to the lobby.

He knew that he didn't have *all* night, that Alba would check on him eventually, around what was supposed to be lights-out time at eleven. But it wasn't close to eleven yet. So he *had* time.

Time to do what?

That was a pretty solid question right there.

He had remembered to take his cell phone with him. If Kate or Alba came up looking for him before eleven and realized he was gone, he knew the first thing they were going to do was call his cell. So he had a cover story ready, that he just had to run to the drugstore for a printer cartridge so he could print the English paper that was due tomorrow. Even though he'd finished the paper two days ago.

So that meant bringing money with him also, in case they called and he did need to run over to the twenty-four-hour Duane Reade on Lexington Avenue and actually *buy* a new printer cartridge.

Zach Harriman, feeling like the new troubleshooter in the family. Except the only trouble tonight was the kind he was making for himself if he got caught.

Pat, one of the night doormen, with his big belly and big Irish accent, was at the security desk when Zach came through the lobby.

"No elevator for ya, young Mr. H.?" he said.

"Getting in shape for b-ball, Pat."

"And where might you be rushin' off to, since I never see ya out by your lonesome at this time a night?"

Zach said, "Homework emergency. Homework 911, Pat. Need to run over to the drugstore and get some school stuff or my English teacher is gonna kill me tomorrow."

Pat said, "You want me to walk with you? I can get Mickey at the back to cover for me a little while."

Zach made himself smile. "Pat," he said. "I'm fourteen, not four."

"Just make sure you're comin' right back, boy-o," Pat said. "I don't want that Alba of yours readin' me the riot act if she calls down wantin' to know if I seen ya."

Zach banged him some fist.

He walked for a long time, north on Fifth, knowing he had walked a mile when he came up on the Metropolitan Museum of Art—twenty blocks equaling roughly a mile in Manhattan.

Zach crossed over to the west side of Fifth now, walked past the incredible entrance to the Met, lit like some kind of movie set.

Zach found himself standing alone at an entrance to Central Park.

He'd never even thought about going in there at night.

Until this night.

Until right now.

And it was real night in there, not some movie set. There was the usual traffic noise behind him, because you got that in New York day or night. People weren't kidding in the song when they said this was the city that never sleeps. But for Zach it was very quiet now, as quiet as the park in front of him.

In or not?

Yes or no?

He felt like there was this fight going on inside him, Zach against Zach.

He took a deep breath, let it out.

And walked away. Turned and walked back across Fifth, not feeling as if he'd wimped out, just feeling as if he wasn't ready. Which brought him back to the same question he'd taken out of the apartment with him and down the steps:

Ready for *what*?

Maybe Kate still knew him, but right now Zach felt as if he didn't know himself anymore.

He walked over to Madison, one block east from Fifth. Then down Madison for a while, usually one of his favorite walking streets in the whole city. Zach was surprised at how many people there were on the sidewalks at this time of night, even with Madison Avenue's shops and stores closed hours ago.

He crossed over to the east side of the block and walked past the Carlyle Hotel, heard singing from inside as the door opened, then heard applause. Zach Harriman, out in the grown-up world, the after-dark big-city world, knowing he should have felt some excitement about it.

But he didn't.

He was walking faster now, heading north again, getting that feeling again, the one he was getting used to: the same one he'd felt the day his dad died, that he had to be somewhere.

He just didn't know where.

It felt as if he was up at 90th and Madison in a blink. He took a left there and headed back toward Central Park, toward his favorite way in, the grand entrance at 90th and Fifth, the long stairway leading to the reservoir.

Zach stopped at the base of the stairs. Feeling the urge to walk up them, not knowing why.

Okay, where you going, dude?

Still not quite sure.

He was wearing his old New Balance gray sneakers. If it were daylight, he would go right up those stairs and start running, a mile and a half, probably do that in under ten minutes if he stepped on it. But he wasn't there now to run laps. Nobody in his right mind ran the res alone at this time of night, unless they were begging to get mugged. Or worse.

But he was sure now that this was where he'd been headed all along.

Zach walked up the stairs.

That was when he saw the guy.

He was about thirty yards to Zach's left. As dark as it was, Zach had no idea how he was able to see him. But he did see him, like he was wearing night-vision glasses.

The guy was crouched in the bushes.

Waiting for something, too. Or someone.

Zach didn't stare. He tried to act like he was invisible. But the guy wasn't watching him, didn't seem to know he'd been spotted. His attention was focused at the far turn, the one that took you into a long straightaway where you could really let it out if you'd run the res counterclockwise and the stairs were your finish line.

There she was. A woman, ponytail bobbing along behind her. Running hard, as if this really was her finish line, maybe thinking she was safe running alone at this time of night because she could outrun anybody.

The guy in the bushes, keeping low, inched out toward the track, still trying to be invisible.

Watching the woman eat up the remaining distance between them. A hundred yards maybe.

Less now.

One of those bad things in the world about to happen to this woman, Zach was sure of it.

And he was the only one around to stop it.

He walked slowly toward the woman. When he got near where the guy was hiding, Zach stopped.

He turned and looked right at him. The guy was in a knit cap and looked to be only a few years older than Zach. His eyes grew wide. Zach could tell he was holding something in his right hand behind him.

He wasn't sure what he was supposed to do, how this was supposed to play out. Wasn't sure, but wasn't scared, either.

It was the other guy who looked scared in that moment, as if Zach had somehow faced him down.

As if the guy had seen something in him.

The footsteps of the woman were close now. Then she said, "Excuse me," because Zach was right in the middle of the track, blocking her way.

So he moved out of the way, turned and watched her run down the steps and across the drive and go right across Fifth Avenue with the light, into the lights of the city.

When Zach looked back into the bushes, the guy was gone.

IF Alba or Kate knew he'd left the apartment that night, neither one of them ever mentioned it. And Zach certainly wasn't going to bring it up, especially not to Kate. He wasn't going to tell her that he'd not only gone in there alone, he'd gotten in the middle of a mugging or managed to scare off a perv or whatever it was he'd done.

But whatever he *had* done, it had felt amazing.

When he'd finally gotten into bed that night, it had taken him what felt like hours to get to sleep, that was how excited he was. How *amped*.

Like he hadn't just faced down his own fears, he'd finally put a face to the Bads and stared them down.

Looked them in the eye and chased *them* off for once.

He had to admit, he did think about going back the next night. And the night after that. But he'd stayed inside the apartment, kept himself busy at his computer. One time he even made it as far as the elevator, feeling those feelings coming up again like a bad moon rising, before he heard his mom, back from her trip by then, say, "Going somewhere?"

Standing there between the foyer and the living room.

Zach was quick enough on his feet to say, "I had a crucial Knicks question for Lenny, but then I remembered like a dope that he's already gone home."

"How about you go back upstairs and focus on some *school* questions," his mom said. "So maybe that B in history becomes the A that it ought to be."

She went back into the living room. Zach followed her, watched her grab her book off the coffee table and settle in on the couch.

"But what if the B is happy being a B?" he said. "What if it turns out that it was an overachieving C before it shocked the world by becoming that B?"

She gave him one of those mother-of-all sighs.

"Be *gone*," she said, pointing up the stairs.

"What if it's that one B that's making all the other B's in the world so darn proud?" he said.

"Go."

He went upstairs and worked on history for a while. When he was done, he went out on the balcony and stared out at the park, wishing his mom hadn't caught him before he could sneak out. He thought about going back on his computer. But he wasn't in the mood to be researching his dad tonight, reading about him instead of talking to him.

He was missing him too much.

That never stopped. That was something he couldn't let go of, the way he couldn't let go of his suspicions— his *belief*—that the accident wasn't actually an accident. There were times when he wanted to talk about it with somebody, with his mom or Kate or *somebody* who wouldn't look at him cross-eyed when he opened up about this stuff. But he hadn't come up with anything beyond his own conspiracy theory.

And the one time he had run it by Kate, she'd acted like she pitied him.

Poor, sad, deluded Zach Harriman.

As much as Kate Paredes loved being right, she was dead wrong about the crash that killed his dad, and one of these days Zach was going to prove it.

And there was no way she understood him and his

feelings, because Zach wasn't close to understanding them himself.

What did he understand on nights like this, clear as the lights of the city in front of him?

His dad was never coming home.

Zach would sit out on the balcony, and for a few minutes he would think this was like all the other missing-dad nights in his life. For a few minutes he would feel exactly the way he used to when his dad was away, and trick himself into thinking he was coming back next week.

But then a much worse feeling would come in right behind it, like he'd been sucker-punched, and he'd remember all over again.

His dad had promised to take him to a Knicks game soon. And over the Christmas break, he had promised they'd go skiing, just the two of them, up in Vermont. All those promises, and more, would never come true now. So that was the emptiest feeling of all.

It was why what should have been good memories now felt like bad ones, because they hurt too much. When his dad used to surprise him and come back early from a trip—no e-mail, no call, no warning—there he'd be, waiting in front of the building when Zach got home from a practice, opening the door with a flourish like he was Lenny the doorman. And whatever age Zach Harriman was at the time, he'd drop his backpack like it was a bad habit and hug his father for all he was worth.

It was as if his dad had some kind of sixth sense, would know exactly when Zach was walking home from Parker, the precise moment when he'd be coming down the street.

Like there was this weird radar between them.

And the next morning, without fail, no matter how jet-lagged his dad should have been, no matter where he'd flown in from, he'd walk Zach—and Kate—to school.

Saying at the front door of Parker: "See you after school, kiddo."

"Swear?" Zach would say.

"On more honor than a whole Boy Scout troop," his dad would say. Before he'd add: "Where else would I be?"

Though they both knew the answer to that one. The correct answer was he could end up almost anywhere, at a moment's notice.

There hadn't been any notice when his dad was finally taken away from him forever. When he was just gone.

The way the old Zach Harriman was gone for good, the one who never wanted to fight back.

His dad used to go off and save the world?

Lately his son just wanted to beat it up.

• • •

Spence Warren wasn't in love with the idea of having Zach Harriman as a teammate on the eighth-grade basketball team at the Parker School.

But then Spence wasn't in love with the idea of Zach sharing the same oxygen he breathed.

Spence played center for Parker, not because he was all that much taller than the rest of the team, but because he was the strongest guy they had. He was also the best athlete on the team and he had a center's mentality.

As much of a total jamoke—another Dad word—as Spence could be everywhere else at Parker, he was a total jock once he got on the court or the playing field. That meant he wanted to win the game. And he knew that for their eighth-grade team to win, Zach's outside shooting needed to be a part of it.

It didn't mean he ever gave Zach a total pass on the court. He'd still make his snarky comments when Zach screwed up a play or missed an open shot, make sure he'd do it in a way that ensured Zach would hear the insult and Coach Piowarski would not. But for the most part, the place where Spence had always tortured Zach the *least* was on a basketball court.

Until today.

Today Spence was messing with Zach's head every chance he got, to the point where Zach thought it was ridiculous to even think about this in terms of *practice*. Because when it came to this kind of chop-busting, Spence didn't need practice, he was practically in the Hall of Fame.

Today he was showing Zach up every chance he could in front of the team, picking his spots like a champ, always managing to do it when Coach P. was looking the other way or talking to somebody else. As usual, Spence had this way of boring in on Zach at his lowest moments, and there had been plenty of those today, because he was totally off his game.

He wasn't off by a lot. But you didn't have to be off by a lot to look like a complete scrub in basketball. He was just a step slow on defense, which meant giving up too many easy baskets and running into one screen after another, ending up on the floor. He ran the wrong way *twice* on one of their basic offensive plays, a play designed to get him an open shot from the corner. Instead of Spence hitting him with a quick pass out of the post, he wound up throwing the ball out of bounds, right past the spot where Zach was supposed to be. After the second time, he glared Zach all the way into the East River for causing another turnover.

Coach P. had seen enough. He blew his whistle, told them to get a drink of water and then come back and see if they could run the play correctly. As Spence ran past Zach, he got into his ear and said, "Hey, is there any chance that if we fly the clue flag today, you might be able to salute it?"

Zach didn't even think of responding. When you were playing like a scrub, you weren't allowed to do anything with trash talk except take it.

Sometimes you even had to take it from the coach, who grinned at Zach as he said, "And this time, let's not have some of us going the wrong way down a one-way street."

It never got better. Zach's head and body just weren't in the game. And now the blue team—the second unit— was beating Zach's red team.

The Reds were down by two points when Spence called a time-out with one minute to go in the fourth. David Epstein had just broken away from Zach for an easy layup. Spence knew what was riding on the last minute because everybody in the gym knew—the losing team had to run after the scrimmage was over. Not just run, but run *suicides.* One of the killer basketball drills of all time. Everybody on the baseline, running fifteen feet and touching the court, then sprinting back to the baseline. Then up to half-court, touching the floor there, coming back. Then the same deal, up to the other foul line, all the way back to the baseline. Finally to the *other* baseline, the full length of the court and back, with whatever legs and wind you had left.

It was a bear of a drill anytime but much, *much* worse after you'd played the equivalent of a full game.

In the huddle, Spence looked right at Zach and said, "*You* are *not* going to be the reason the rest of us have to run today.

"Your girlfriend would be doing more for us today than you are," Spence continued, red-faced. "Maybe we can get her out of play practice before we're all on the baseline and Coach starts blowing his stupid whistle."

"Leave her out of it," Zach said in a quiet voice, not even looking at him. "This one's on *me*."

"How 'bout you get on your *man*, freak boy," Spence said, "and look like an actual starter for at least one minute today?"

Zach knew he was right. And he did try as hard as he could during that last minute. Tried so hard that he forced a bullet pass into Spence that was too low and too hard to handle. The pass bounced off his knee and right into the blue center's hands. He looked up and saw a wide-open David Epstein streaking toward the basket, completely uncovered.

Last two points of the game.

Coach P. blew his whistle and said, "Tragically, the

reds must go and line up now, because apparently our second unit is stronger than our starters."

"Because of one guy?" Spence said.

"Hey," Coach said, "you know my philosophy. It's never one play that loses a game and it's never one guy."

Spence made a point of getting next to Zach.

"Sorry about comparing you to a girl," he said under his breath. "'Cause if you think about it, that's really, *really* insulting to girls."

Coach blew his whistle. And the red team ran. And ran some more.

When they were finished, all of them totally gassed, Coach told Zach and Spence to pick up the balls.

Sweet, Zach thought. *More alone time with my best friend in the world.*

Spence picked up the balls, tossed them to Zach, who put them on the rolling rack. Neither one of them said anything until Zach said, "You take off, I'll put them in the storage room."

He was nearly to the gym's double doors when the ball Spence Warren whipped at him hit him on the back of his head.

Zach stumbled forward into the rack of balls, which went bouncing away from him. When he wheeled around, the back of his head stinging like he'd been slapped,

Spence had his hand up, the way guys in tennis did after they'd gotten a fluke winner off the top of the net.

"Sorry," Spence said, grinning at him. "Thought you were looking."

Fifteen minutes later Zach *was* looking.

Looking for Spence.

ZACH took the stairs down to the front door of the school. But instead of walking down Madison in the direction of his apartment building, he walked over to Fifth Avenue, crossed the street and went into Central Park.

Spence, he knew, lived on Central Park West, over on the other side of the park. Spence had proudly pointed out the building one day last spring when their class had taken the short bus ride over to the West Side, a field trip to see some tall ships cruising their way down the Hudson River. Spence, of course, acted as if he owned the entire building.

Zach knew that if you entered the park at 86th Street, it was practically a straight shot to Spence's building. So this had to be his way home.

Maybe the old Zach would have let this go, not just the ball hitting him in the head, a cheap shot if there ever was one, but the entire way Spence had acted at practice today. Ragging on him every time he saw an opening. And even when he didn't.

The new Zach wasn't letting it go.

If he could come into this place at night and scare off a mugger, he could do this with Spence once and for all. Still plenty of daylight left. Coach P. made sure practice started at two-thirty sharp every day so that the kids who lived close enough to Parker to walk to school—or the ones who took the subway home—could get home when it was still light out.

There.

He saw Spence coming.

Listening to his iPod, earbuds in his ears, bopping his head to music Zach couldn't hear.

Zach hadn't imagined the scene playing out this way. He'd pictured himself calling out Spence's name, getting his attention, telling him they needed to have a talk.

Only now Spence wouldn't be able to hear him.

So Zach ran up ahead and hopped the stone wall. He was waiting for Spence as he came around a bend in Park Drive, planning to jump out at him the way the guy at the reservoir had been planning to surprise that woman jogger the other night.

Not quite.

Spence noticed him and shook his head, more an-noyed or just plain disgusted than surprised. He pulled out his white earbuds.

"*What?*" he said.

"What?" Zach said. "You're not happy to see me?"

"Harriman," Spence said, "as much fun as it is to jack you up from time to time—"

He started to pass, but Zach blocked his way.

"Time to time?" Zach said. Trying to grin a Spence grin back at him. "Don't you mean *all* the time?"

"I *don't* have the time for it today. My mom is waiting for me at home. We gotta do something. As a family." Air-quoting the word *family*.

"Well," Zach said, "even though I hate cutting into your *family* time, we need to talk."

"About what?"

"About you being an even bigger jerk than I thought you were," Zach said. "Which, I have to say, would make you the biggest pain-in-the-butt jerk our age in history. Like we should be studying jerks like you in one of our *history* books."

Spence tilted his head, as if this were another time he couldn't possibly have heard right.

"You must be joking, freak boy."

Zach shook his head. "No, you heard me," he said.

"But *you're* not hearing *me,*" Spence said. "I don't have time for this."

"Make time, Spence."

"If I do," Spence said, "that ball hitting you on the head is going to feel like a love tap."

"I doubt it."

Zach wasn't even thinking about what he wanted to say, the words just kept coming out like he was the coolest, toughest guy in the park.

"Okay, then," Spence said, shrugging. "Let's do this."

"Let's."

Zach turned and hopped back over the wall, leading the way. Spence was a few yards behind, speaking quietly into his cell phone, Zach hearing him tell somebody that he was ten minutes away, swear.

Zach had already picked out the spot beforehand, a small clearing between a patch of trees at the top of a hill. He could see a touch football game being played, the shouts and laughter reaching him. Even now, even with what was about to happen between him and Spence, Zach couldn't help thinking what a big, amazing place Central Park was, how there was a different kind of show going on inside it every hundred yards.

Including this one. Just the two of them.

Zach hadn't dropped his backpack on the ground yet.

He knew and Spence knew that once he did, it was of-ficially on between them, no turning back.

"Is this about me hitting you with the ball?" Spence said. "Get over it. You sucked up the joint today and you know it."

"Actually it's about everything, Spence," Zach said. "Mostly it's about you being you, the way you are with me. That ends today."

"Does it?"

"Yeah," Zach said. "It does."

Spence grinned, almost like he was enjoying this now. Of course he was. No way he wanted to change the way things were between them. He enjoyed torturing Zach way too much for that.

"Who's gonna make it end?"

"I am," Zach said.

Zach shrugged off his backpack, let it drop to the ground. As he did, almost in the same motion, he turned and started to throw the first punch he had ever thrown at another person in his life.

He threw it like this one punch could take out all the Bads at once because, let's face it, if he was looking to put a face on them, Spence's would sure do.

He hit nothing but air.

And then the air was coming out of him.

It turned out Spence wasn't looking to have a fistfight with him or fight by Zach's rules, that he hadn't even needed to throw a punch. No, Spence the football player had dropped his shoulder and drove it into him, making Zach feel as if his insides were exploding.

As soon as he'd opened up to throw his punch, he was as defenseless as a quarterback was in football right after he released the ball. And Spence was the same star linebacker he was for the Parker School, driving Zach back and taking him down, nothing to break Zach's fall as he went down hard into the grass and dirt, his head hitting first.

Spence had been right about one thing.

The basketball hitting him did feel like a love tap now.

There was no chance for Zach to fight back because he couldn't even *breathe.* Spence was on top of him, his knee planted firmly into his stomach.

"You wanted to have a fight?" Spence said. He was breathing heavily, his face red, eyes big. "Well, now we're having a fight."

He grabbed the front of Zach's hoodie, then slammed him back into the ground.

"How do you think the judges are scoring it so far?" Spence said.

Spence pulled back *his* fist now, ready to end this with one punch of his own.

That's when his cell went off.

The ring tone was a rap song, one Zach didn't recognize. But it stopped Spence, made him look at his clenched fist, frozen there in midair.

Slowly he pulled his hand down and reached for his phone. Looked to see who was calling. Answered it. Nodded as he heard the voice at the other end of the call.

"Mom," he said. "I'm practically just crossing the street."

Even a bully like Spence was somebody's kid.

He didn't punch Zach when he snapped the phone shut, just picked him up again, dropping him this time the way you would dirty clothes.

Got up and stood over him.

"Gotta ask you something, Harriman," he said. "You sure he was your dad?"

Saving the hardest hit for last.

HIS dad had always told him that fighting only proved who was the better fighter, and usually you knew that before you started.

Maybe that was another reason why it was over before it started. Or maybe Spence had proved that he was better at Ultimate Fighting, putting a shoulder into Zach and putting him on his back before he knew what was happening.

Zach's pride had been hurt, that was for sure. And the back of his head hurt a lot, from when it had hit the ground. The good news? There wasn't a mark on him, at least on the outside.

Inside was another matter.

Inside hurt as much as the comment about his dad

had. Because when Spence took him down as easily as knocking over a toy soldier, it was as if he'd knocked Zach all the way back to the kid he used to be.

The kid who would never have had the rope to take on Spence in the first place.

But because there weren't any bruises, he didn't have to explain anything to anybody. After dinner he and Kate went to his room to work on a history project, comparing President Franklin Roosevelt's first term with President Addison's.

"How'd practice go today?" Kate said.

"Fine. But what does that have to do with the New Deal, exactly?" he said.

"Not a thing," she said. "I can help you work on our project and talk about something else entirely at the same time. It's called multitasking, Harriman. One of my specialties."

"One of your many."

"I was about to point that out myself."

"Tragically," he said, "I know."

"Oh, here we go, how full of myself am I?"

"Well," Zach said, grinning. "Maybe not *full*. But let's just say you don't leave much room for dessert."

She punched him. "I can't tell sometimes," she said. "Are you my biggest fan or my biggest critic?"

"I can be both. It's called multitasking."

"Touché," she said. She closed her history book. "So what about practice?"

"Practice was practice. Why do you suddenly care so much about it?"

"I just noticed you were pretty quiet at dinner."

"I know this is going to sound crazy," he said. "But when I don't have something to say, I don't talk."

He actually did have something he wanted to say to her. It just wasn't about basketball practice, and this didn't feel like the right moment.

"Look out tomorrow night," Zach said. "You probably won't be able to shut me up."

"Liar."

"You call me that a lot lately."

"Because you're keeping things from me."

"So you say."

"No, Harriman, I *know*. And if you want to say that's just me being a pushy know-it-all, have at it. I'm not stopping you. But I know *something* happened today after I saw you in last period, whether it had to do with basketball or something else."

She *was* good sometimes. A *lot* of times. But Zach wasn't caving. Or giving her the satisfaction of knowing she was right. Somehow telling her about the fight with Spence would have felt like getting knocked down all over again.

"Sometimes you're wrong," he said.

"I know that."

Zach threw up his hands. "Only you can act right about being wrong!"

"Go ahead if you want, change the subject."

Why not? Zach thought. Why not try it out on Kate before he approached his mom with it? He needed someone to know.

"I've been thinking," he said.

"Uh-oh," Kate said, grinning, and made a move like she wanted to hide under the bed.

"Seriously," he said. Took a deep breath, let it out. Then let it rip. "You want to know what's up? Here it is. I'm thinking I might want to go and look at the crash site. You know, just to check it out for myself."

Kate surprised him. She didn't say anything right away. Just stared off, like she was processing the information. Finally she said, "It's not a crash site anymore, Harriman. It's just a big old empty field near some bay out there, before you get to the ocean."

"I never saw it with my own eyes," he said. "And I'd just like to, that's all."

"And if you do, what then? You'll let it go, game over, the conspiracy stuff?"

"Yes."

"Or are you going out there because you've convinced

yourself there's some clue that's just waiting to be discovered by you?"

Zach didn't know if she meant it to come out as sar-
castic as it did. But that's the way he heard it. He *did*
think back to practice now, Spence using the same tone
of voice when he offered to fly the clue flag for him.

"And what if I did think that? You'd think that's
funny?"

"I didn't say I thought it was funny—"

"Because," Zach said, "if you do think it's funny, then
you don't know me nearly as well as you think you do."

Another time when he was hot, just like that.

"Maybe I don't," Kate said.

She started collecting her books and pens and stood
up, her way of telling him they were done here.

"Sorry I brought it up," he said.

"Why?"

"Why am I sorry?"

Kate said, "No, why can't you give this up, stop thinking you're Sherlock Harriman or something?"

It was like she was asking all the questions he couldn't
answer himself these days, about why he'd go into the
park at night or why he'd pick a fight with Spence.

Why he sometimes felt as if somebody else was at the
controls of his life.

"I just can't," he said.

She turned to leave, then stopped herself.

"When you want to tell me what's really going on," she said, "you can. But I can see you're not ready to do that. And you're *not* yourself right now."

Then she left, the girl who just had to be right not knowing how right she really was.

When he came home from basketball practice the next day, he decided he wasn't going to wait any longer. He was going to come right out with it to his mom, ask her straight up to take him out to where the plane had gone down.

It was almost as far out as you could go on eastern Long Island, not too far from what was known as Land's End. Past towns like Bridgehampton, East Hampton, Amagansett and Montauk. Zach had asked his dad once what comes after Montauk.

"Portugal," his dad had said with a grin. "After a whole lot of ocean."

Zach was hoping his mom would be alone when he got home. But when he came out of the elevator and around the corner to the living room, he saw that Uncle John was with her.

Not such a bad thing, he thought.

Because John Marshall really was like a favorite uncle, the one who pretty much always took your side or let you do whatever you wanted. Or, better yet, *gets* you what you want. It was like that even when Zach's dad was alive. Whenever Zach wanted to get something from his parents—or get something out of them—he went straight to Uncle John, knowing he'd have his back.

It was just another reason why Zach had never thought of him as their family lawyer. Or as an uncle, really. He was more like an older friend, one with serious connections, his dad's best friend since Harvard, his roommate there, his football teammate, then his lawyer and wingman for life.

He had a deep voice and looked a little bit like Liam Neeson, the actor, and it was as if he'd been smiling at Zach for Zach's whole life. Like the two of them were sharing some kind of inside joke.

If Uncle John was over for dinner, Zach knew he could get an extra hour added on to his bedtime. If Zach wanted a new Fathead poster for his room and Uncle John found out about it, done deal. Or a quick trip to Carvel on Lexington with Kate while the grown-ups had coffee after dinner.

"I never had children of my own to spoil," Uncle John had said to him one time. "So I guess I'll have to spoil you, Zachary."

He'd always called him that. Not Zach, like everyone else.

Zachary.

Zach had said, "I can take it."

And John Marshall had smiled and said, "Be brave, Zachary. Be brave."

Today Uncle John and his mom looked to be having afternoon tea. Elizabeth Harriman took one look at Zach and said, "Shower. Now."

"Can't I even say hello to Uncle John?" he said. "Seriously, Mom. Where are your manners?"

Uncle John said, "How's the outside shot, Zachary?"

"Getting there. Slowly. *Extremely* slowly."

"Squaring up the shoulders?"

"When I do, my shot's wet."

"Great," his mom said. "Now you go get wet. *In the shower.*"

"Need to ask you something before I do."

"Make it fast," she said. "I love you more than life itself, but even from over here you smell like feet."

They were on the couch. Zach took a seat across from them, on the other side of an antique coffee table. John Marshall, as always, was in a dark suit and white shirt and striped tie. Black shoes, shined up and looking brand new.

"Must be serious," Uncle John said. "The boy sits."

He told them then. Not just directing it at his mom. At both of them. Throwing in a little Dr. Abbott–speak at the end, saying that he'd been thinking about it a lot and it was the only way for him to get closure, by seeing where the accident had happened.

His mom didn't take as long to react as Kate had.

"No," she said.

"But Mom . . ."

"No 'but Mom,'" she said. "I went out there after it happened. Once was enough, believe me."

"But at least you went once," Zach said.

"It's not a trip I wanted to make," she said. "Or one you're going to."

"This is something you've been thinking about a lot, haven't you?" asked Uncle John.

"Well, yeah," Zach said. "It's not like I'm fixed on it. Or it's something I really *want* to do. But it's something I feel like I *have* to do."

"Perhaps as a way of feeling some kind of connection to your father?" John Marshall said.

"Hey," Zach's mom said. "Whose side are you on here?"

He patted her on the knee but continued speaking to Zach. "It's something like that, isn't it?"

Zach said, "I hadn't thought about it that way, but yeah, maybe it is."

Go with it. It was like Uncle John was passing him the ball, setting up an open jump shot.

"Think about it however you want," his mom said. "Both of you. The answer is still no. You're not putting yourself through that, no matter how swell of an idea you think it is. And I'm not going back there, end of story, end of conversation."

"If you don't want to, I understand, I wouldn't make you," Zach said. "So let Alba take me out on the Jitney." The Jitney was this cool bus people took from New York City out to the Hamptons. Zach and Kate had taken it a few times, loving life on it because it even featured wireless Internet service.

"Sorry, pal, but this conversation really is over," Elizabeth Harriman said.

She could be the nicest, coolest, most understanding mom in the world. But when she dug in like this, Zach knew, you had a better chance of moving Madison Square Garden across Seventh Avenue.

"Let the boy do it," Uncle John said. "Let him go there and be there and then be done with it. If you don't, this will continue to be an itch he can't scratch. And the discussion won't end here; it will go on and on. And on."

"John *Marshall*," she said. "You know how much I respect your opinion. And how much I rely on your wisdom for all things relating to the welfare of this family. Just not this time."

She gave him a look that Zach was pretty sure you

wouldn't have been able to dent with a hammer. Then she looked back at Zach and took an epic deep breath. "Maybe the next time we're out on the island, whenever that is, *maybe* the two of us can take a drive out there one day. But for now, when the healing has barely begun, I don't want you to do this. So you're *not* doing this."

Zach opened his mouth and closed it.

He thought, *Healing?* Was she kidding? What, she'd managed to patch up the hole in the universe his dad had fallen through and not mentioned that to anybody?

"I hear you," he said to his mom.

He got up out of his chair, told Uncle John he'd see him and left them there with their tea and what he was sure was going to be a pretty lively conversation.

He hadn't even made it up the first stair before the realization hit him.

He was making the trip out to Land's End. On his own.

HE waited until Saturday morning, just because it would have been too complicated to pull off on a school day.

He and Kate were supposed to stop at the New York Public Library, the big branch, on 42nd Street, for a couple of books they needed on FDR. From there they were going to a one o'clock Knicks game, because Uncle John had scored them some prime tickets.

It would be the first Knicks game for him since his dad died.

Zach and Kate planned to take the Lexington Avenue subway down to the library, then just walk the rest of the way to the Garden. After the game they were going to stop at the ESPN Zone in Times Square, have a soda, maybe go to the third floor and play some of the games.

It was when they were about to walk down the steps at the 68th Street station, the Hunter College stop, that Zach told her. Having waited as long as he could.

"I need a favor," he said. "A big one. Gi-gundo, in fact."

"You got it," Kate said.

She had her hair in a ponytail that came out through the opening of her favorite Knicks trucker cap. He knew she was wearing her David Lee No. 42 jersey under her parka.

"You might not want to say that when you know what the favor is."

"Don't have to know."

"Okay, then I need you to cover for me," he said. "I'm not going downtown with you. I'm going to take the Jitney out to Montauk."

She pulled her cap down so low he could barely see her face now.

"But your mom said no," Kate said.

"I know."

"And you're going anyway?"

"Yeah."

She looked up and surprised him then. "I'm going with you."

"You don't want me to go any more than my mom does."

"But if you're going, and I can see you're fixed on going or you wouldn't have given me hardly any time to talk you out of this, then I'm not letting you go alone."

"Thank you," Zach said. "But no."

"Why not?"

"Because the more I've thought about it, I'm almost glad Mom said no, 'cause this is something I need to do alone," he said. "So just cover for me. Please, Katie. If I catch the next bus, I can get out there and get back by the time we're due home."

She shook her head. "We could go together and get back together and it'd be pretty much the same deal."

Zach grinned. "I know you can out-debate me on stuff. *Most* stuff. Just don't out-debate me today, okay?"

"What if you get back late? Then what do I tell your mom?"

"You're Kate the Great," he said. "You'll think of something."

She said, "You don't have to do this even though you think you do. You can call it off right now and we can get on the train."

"No," he said. "I do have to do it. But I can't without your help."

"Just because I don't agree with you doesn't mean I'm not *with* you." She pulled her cell out of the side pocket of her parka and held it up, like she was trying to sell it to him. "Four bars, fully charged," she said. "I want calls or texts throughout the day. You don't make a move out there without me knowing about it. Understood?"

He nodded. "I know better than to cross you," he said. "It's worse than crossing Jack Bauer."

"Go get on the bus," she said.

He did.

There was hardly any traffic going out on a Saturday morning and the Jitney was only half full, which made it seem even more quiet than usual. People were sleeping or reading or listening to their iPods. Zach had the longest trip, all the way to Montauk, about three hours out with no bad traffic.

It meant a six-hour round-trip. Plenty of time for him to get back to the city, meet up with Kate, be home for dinner the way they'd promised.

In the past he'd sometimes fallen asleep on the Jitney. But today he was too wired, wanting the driver to go faster, wanting to be out there right now. He looked out the window once they were on the Long Island Expressway, watched the exit signs go by way too slowly, Douglaston and Great Neck, Melville, Commack, Port Jefferson and Yaphank.

When the bus got off at Exit 70, Zach knew it was just about an hour from there to the last stop in Montauk.

They made their way on Route 27 through all the towns Zach knew by heart, all the stops before Portugal. East Hampton finally gave way to Amagansett. He was close now, feeling it without having to look at any signs.

He had brought money with him. When he got into Montauk, he called the number of the taxi service he'd looked up the night before, knowing the crash site was too far for him to walk to from town.

When the driver showed up a few minutes later, Zach gave him the address.

The driver said, "There's nothing out there but water and sky, kid."

"There's some other stuff," Zach said.

"It's your dollar. But I don't feel right leaving a kid out in the middle of nowhere by himself."

"Do you have a card with your number on it?" Zach said. "I'll call you when I'm ready to come back to town."

The driver handed him a card. "Your parents know where you are?"

"Oh, yeah," Zach said. "And I'm from here." As if that explained everything to the guy, like being a local was the same as having a signed permission slip.

As they drove away from town, Zach started to have the same strange feeling he'd had since he'd gotten up this morning, even before he was on the bus. The feeling that he was supposed to be doing this, supposed to be here.

Or maybe this was just one more way for Zach to test himself.

By the time the taxi pulled over to the side of the road, near the field where the plane had gone down, between the bay and the ocean, it really did look like Land's End. Zach paid the man, watched the taxi turn around and head back toward town and felt as if he'd been dropped off at the end of the world.

He texted Kate.

Im here.

As he was crossing the narrow road, her reply came back so quickly it was as if she were returning one of his shots in tennis.

B careful.

But it made him think of something his dad used to say to him all the time:

Be careful what you wish for.

He had wanted to come here. Wanted in some way to find his dad out here. Only now that he *was* here, he felt more alone than ever, small under the big sky you always saw when you got close to the ocean.

There wasn't a house or building in sight.

He made his way through some tall grass and into the field, noticing some yellow police tape that had been left behind, like trash. It was like a sign that he was getting close to the place where the plane had fallen out of the sky, for reasons nobody had ever explained.

"Look to the sky," his dad used to tell Zach when he was little and wondering what he would be when he grew up. "Look to the sky." Well, the sky was empty now. The sky had betrayed him.

It took maybe a hundred yards more, and then he was there. In just about every news story Zach had read about the crash of Tom Harriman's plane, they had talked about the "scorched" earth the first responders had found.

Finally he could see with his own eyes what they meant.

Around the hole in the ground where the nose of the plane must have hit, it looked as if someone had set fire to this field. And all around Zach could see other reminders of what the day must have been like: tire tracks in the mud that the police cars and emergency vehicles had left, more burnt and trampled grass.

Zach Harriman knew how much his dad loved flying, knew how much pride he took in it. He had been almost cocky about his ability to pilot a plane, talking about how he welcomed bad weather because that was "real flying." When that pilot had landed the US Airways flight on the Hudson River, Tom Harriman and Zach had watched the highlights all day and all night and at one point his dad had said, "I'm jealous."

"Jealous?" Zach had said.

"Yeah," his dad had said. "That Sully got to make that landing instead of me."

Zach walked a big circle around what Kate had said wasn't a crash site anymore, but was. Not knowing what he was looking for, still wanting answers. Looking around and realizing there was no one around here to give him any. He noticed that even though it was early afternoon, the sky had grown dark, as if a storm might be on its way from the ocean.

The wind picked up, starting to howl.

Maybe his mom had been right. Maybe there was nothing out here worth seeing.

Zach had been angry since the crash, angry every day. But today he just felt sad, sad that he'd built this trip up so much in his mind, sad that he'd set himself up for this kind of letdown.

He walked away from the hole in the ground, toward the ocean, thinking he would soon come to the end of the field, some kind of fence or boundary. But he didn't. He'd been able to hear the ocean when he'd first gotten out of the taxi, but not now. Now there was just the wind drowning out everything else.

The sky turned even darker.

Okay, I'm out of here, Zach thought, *before this turns into the twister scene from* The Wizard of Oz.

One more look at the hole in the ground, then he'd call the number on the back of the driver's card. He hadn't found anything, certainly not anything resembling a clue. But at least he'd come. At least he didn't have to wonder anymore.

He walked back the way he'd come, arrived at the hole, knelt in the ruined grass, grabbed a fistful of dirt. For some reason he imagined his dad watching him now, from somewhere, from wherever heaven was, being proud of him for doing this.

Zach said good-bye to him.

He tossed the dirt away and started to get up, then stopped, because, as dark as it had grown, he saw a flash of light, reflecting off something.

Zach reached down and pushed the dirt away.

Felt the breath come out of him all at once.

Knowing what he was looking at the way he knew the password for his computer. Or the combination to his locker.

Or his dad's face.

A Morgan silver dollar.

And not just any Morgan, Zach knew.

He knew of only two.

There was the one he was holding in the palm of his

hand now and the one back home in the apartment, in his room, on the shelf above his bed. That's where he kept it when he wasn't trying to squeeze good luck out of it.

This was the one his dad carried with him wherever he went, to all the bad places. To this bad place.

Zach rubbed it against his jacket and then spit on his hand and cleaned it up a little more. His dad's Morgan, no question. It was an 1879 and when he'd given one to Zach on his eighth birthday, he'd given this one to himself at the same time. Told Zach that day that from now on if he squeezed it hard enough, Tom Harriman would know, no matter where he was or what he was doing.

So Zach squeezed.

"I've been waiting for you," a voice said.

THE old man wasn't much taller than Zach. He had snow white hair, a lot of it, and a wispy white beard to go with it.

He was wearing faded jeans and one of those old leather bomber jackets that hung on him a bit, as if it were a size too large. A plain gray sweatshirt showed underneath it, and he had on a pair of old Reebok sneakers that looked older than he was.

He was smiling, maybe as a way of telling Zach not to be afraid. Like that was going to work.

"What do you think you're doing, sneaking up on me like that?" Zach shouted.

"Didn't think I was," the old man said.

"Well, you're wrong."

"Calm down, Zach," the old man said. "I'm sorry I scared you."

"You didn't scare me," Zach said. "And how do you know my name?"

"Friend of the family," the old man said.

He smiled again, put out his hand. Zach ignored it.

"Then how come I don't know you?"

"Simple. You weren't ready yet."

"Ready for what?"

"For you to know me the way I know you."

It had taken all of a minute for Zach to feel as if he were walking in circles, even standing still.

"You said you'd been waiting for me?" Zach said.

"So I did. And so I have."

"You haven't told me *your* name."

"Call me Mr. Herbert."

"Okay, Mr. Herbert. You live around here?"

The old man shook his head. "I was just out here observing, I guess you could say."

"How come I didn't see you before this?"

"Because I didn't want to, Zacman."

It startled him. Only his dad had ever called him Zacman. Ever. It had started as a joke, because when he was little, Zach was always eating on the run.

"I don't need Pacman," his dad had said to him one time. "I've got my very own Zacman."

It had stuck. For his dad, anyway. No one else had ever called him that.

"Don't call me that," Zach said now.

"I'm sorry. I know that was your dad's nickname for you," the old man said. "Like I told you, kid. I'm a friend of the family."

"Who's been waiting for me out here."

"Correct."

He thought of the way the taxi driver had described this place. "The middle of nowhere."

For some reason, Zach flashed to all the times he'd been told not to talk to strangers, the way all kids are told that from the time they're old enough to walk out of their parents' sight. Now here he was with this perfect stranger, this old man who seemed to know way too much about him.

And who talked in riddles.

"You keep saying you're a friend of the family," Zach said. "But I don't recall my dad ever mentioning a friend of his named Mr. Herbert."

"No reason for him to. There was a lot your dad never told you about himself. Am I right, Zacman?"

"I told you: stop calling me Zacman."

"As you wish." Mr. Herbert smiled. "And you can put the coin away; I promise I won't steal it."

Zach looked down, opened his hand, as if to make sure the Morgan was still there. He said, "How did you know . . . ?"

"Because I know about *you,*" Mr. Herbert said. "It's what I'm trying to tell you. I know about your father's death and I know about your life." His eyes darted all around as he nodded. "A life that we both know is changing faster than the weather."

Zach stared at him. This old man who not only knew what was in his hand, but what was in *him.* He thought about turning and running, getting away from him right now, but knew he wouldn't.

Knew that somehow Mr. Herbert was the reason why he was here.

"There are things you need to know about your father," Mr. Herbert said.

"Like what?"

"Like how much of his life was a lie," the old man said.

A blast of wind nearly knocked both of them over as a huge thunderclap boomed from out east, over the water.

"My father didn't lie," Zach said. "Ever."

"That may be a matter of opinion."

"What do you want from me, Mr. Herbert?"

"Let's start by taking a walk."

He started to put a hand on Zach's shoulder. Zach leaned away from it, like a boxer pulling back from a punch. The old man shrugged and made a gesture that said, follow me. Zach did, a few steps behind.

Maybe fifty yards from where the plane had hit, on the bay end of the field, was a stone wall he hadn't even noticed. The old man sat down when he came to it, patted a spot next to him.

"Just a second," Zach said, and pulled out his cell, checking the time on it. One-twenty. He couldn't chase Mr. Herbert around this conversation forever, like chasing him around a video game. Or through a maze. The Jitney was scheduled to go back to Manhattan at two o'clock.

He thought about texting Kate. . . .

"Call her if you want," Mr. Herbert said. "Won't bother me. I was sort of hoping you'd bring her along."

"How did you know . . . ?"

"You're starting to sound like a broken record, boy."

"So you know Kate, too?"

"In a manner of speaking."

"And I suppose you know Alba, and Uncle John?"

The old man smirked. "Even your buddy Spence."

Zach thought: *It's like he's been following me.*

He said, "Were you here the day the plane crashed? Did you see it happen?"

"Didn't need to," Mr. Herbert said. "What happened to him had been happening for a long time, and he was the only one who didn't see it. On either side of the fight."

"What does *that* mean?" Zach said. "You either saw the crash or you didn't."

"And the thing is, I tried to warn him."

"You tried to warn him," Zach said. "About what, exactly?"

"You ever hear the expression about people starting to believe their own press clippings? That's what started to happen to your father."

"You're telling me that my dad did something that *caused* this to happen?"

The old man paused a beat before answering.

"In a way, yes."

Zach Harriman was starting to get dizzy now, trying to keep up with this, all of it swarming around him like flies.

Mr. Herbert said, "It wasn't just one thing, mind you. It was a lot of things, over a lot of years. Almost like he was another very smart guy accumulating too much debt."

"Listen," Zach said, "I have to get back to the city soon. So if you know something about my dad's accident— even though I don't think it was an accident—how about you just tell me."

"You're not ready for that yet," the old man said. "You're closer than you used to be, a lot closer. But still not there."

Zach started to say something smart back to him, but the old man held up a hand, stopping him. "And there are things I could tell you, about both your father and yourself, that you need to find out for yourself. That's the way it worked for him and that's the way it has to work for you. The only way."

"I wish I knew what the heck you were talking about," Zach said. "But I don't. And I don't have any more time for this."

Another smile. "Actually you do. Trust me."

"Trust *you*?" Zach said. "I don't have any idea who you are, really. Or if Mr. Herbert is even your name. Or if you really knew my dad at all."

The old man put out his hand. "Let me see the coin for a second," he said.

Something about the casual way he asked made Zach do it. Zach unclenched his fist, held his palm open and handed it over.

And when it was in the old man's hand, it was as if a

switch had been thrown, the coin suddenly as bright and brilliant as some kind of neon light.

Almost like the Morgan was on fire.

The old man's face was lit by it, too.

"You should trust me because I was the one who first told your father he had the magic in him," Mr. Herbert said.

He tried to hand the coin back to Zach, but Zach pulled his hand away, as if touching it would be like touching a hot stove.

"Don't be afraid, boy," the old man said. "You've got the magic, too."

He flipped the coin in the air between them and Zach caught it.

Then the old man turned and began walking away.

MAGIC?

What did *that* mean?

Zach knew he couldn't just let the old man walk away like this, not knowing if he'd ever see him again. He'd come here looking for answers and now he had what felt like a hundred more questions.

"*Wait!*"

The old man was moving faster than Zach expected, away from the crash site, deeper into the field, about to disappear into grass as tall as he was, grass that seemed to have sprung up while they'd been talking.

Zach ran after him, pulling out his cell, seeing that it

was one-thirty already, knowing that his chance of making the two o'clock bus was disappearing as fast as Mr.
Herbert.

And then, just like that, the old man was gone.

Impossible, Zach thought.

He had only looked down at the phone for a second,
long enough to check the time.

He ran harder to where he had last seen Mr. Herbert.
Zach ran as though there was an engine inside him,
propelling him, yet one more time he felt out of control,
chasing the unknown. Only, this time, the need made
him feel almost desperate.

Not life and death.

But close enough.

He had to find this old man, had to find the one person who seemed to know the changes that had been
taking place inside him.

Who claimed to know his father and how he'd died.

*"I was the one who first told your father he had the
magic in him."*

Zach ran through the high grass toward the water,
toward the darkest part of the sky, the Morgan trying to
burn a hole in the palm of his hand.

He ran, ignoring the high grass as it whipped him
across the face, feeling as if all the wind of the day were
at his back now. Closed his eyes and ran, faster. Feeling

like he was the one flying now, across this field where his father had crashed.

Like he'd become invisible.

When he opened his eyes—like he was coming out of some kind of dream—Zach saw that he was now running across the Sheep Meadow in Central Park.

Saw that he was home.

But . . . *how?*

Zach leaned against a tree, out of breath, put the Morgan dollar in his pocket and pulled out his cell phone.

One-thirty. The same time he had seen when he was still trying to make the two o'clock bus more than a hundred miles from here.

As if he had texted himself home.

As if by magic.

HE started walking down Fifth Avenue, toward home, before remembering he couldn't show up there without Kate, and the Knicks game wasn't close to being over yet. Tip-off had been at one, which meant the second quarter was just about to begin.

Maybe I should just text myself over to the Garden, Zach thought.

See if he could make himself appear at the corner of 33rd and Seventh the way he had in Central Park.

Thinking: *Okay, this is seriously weird.*

Something had just happened to him. Something that the old man said connected Zach to his dad. Something that made no sense, not in the real world anyway.

"Don't be afraid, boy," the old man had said to him. "You've got the magic, too."

Like this was the movies, or TV, like he was in that show *Heroes* he used to watch. Or had climbed into an old Fantastic Four comic book.

Yet he wasn't made up. And this was no movie.

Could he really have powers?

He needed to talk with Kate. Needed the power of *her*.

No secrets between them on this. Tell her everything, leave out nothing, hope that she didn't think he'd lost his mind. Ask her to help him figure out what it all meant.

He needed to see her right now, prove to her that he was back in the city and not still out on the island getting ready to board that two o'clock bus.

Zach reached into his pocket. Not the one with the Morgan dollar inside it, his other pocket. Found the ticket to the Knicks he'd left there. He'd offered it to Kate before he left, telling her she could ask somebody else to go to the game with her.

She'd given him a look and said, "What, and blow your cover?"

Zach didn't run this time, downtown and then crosstown to the Garden. He used conventional transportation, putting his hand up and hailing a New York City taxi and saying the words his dad used to let him say:

"Take me to the Garden."

Once, saying that had seemed like all the magic he'd needed.

He didn't text Kate on the way or call to tell her he was coming. Zach didn't completely understand why he wanted to surprise her, but he did. Just be there next to her when she turned around.

He got out of the taxi in front of the Garden marquee on Seventh, walked through the lobby with its huge color photographs of current Knick players, past the mural showing all the great Garden athletes of the past, handed his ticket to the man at the turnstiles and went up the escalator to the floor of the arena, hearing his first cheers from inside as he got closer to the game.

Usually his excitement at being at the Garden would start as soon as he walked in off the street, but not today. Today the excitement was knowing he was about to see Kate and have her see him, that he had something even more amazing to show her than a Wilson Chandler dunk.

He kept showing ushers his ticket, telling them he knew where his seat was. As he made his way down toward it, he looked up at the clock above the court, saw there were four minutes left in the first half. David Lee was at the free throw line.

When he got close, he spotted Kate's ponytail, saw her leaning forward, all of her energy—Zach sometimes thought you could light their whole building with it— focused on her man, Lee.

Who made the first free throw.

"How's the game?" Zach said, not waiting, sitting down next to her.

She was as startled as Zach had been by Mr. Herbert, like she was seeing a ghost.

"Whoa," she said.

"Whoa yourself."

"You can't be here," she said, eyes big.

"I know."

"Oh, good, as long as you know."

"Not only do I know. I can explain."

David Lee made his second free throw and the crowd cheered. The Celtics called a time-out. The Knicks City Dancers came out to perform one of their numbers to some hip-hop music Zach vaguely recognized, music exploding from everywhere as if everything underneath the spoked Garden ceiling had turned into a giant boom box.

"You *cannot* explain how you made it all the way to the Hamptons and back by now," Kate said over the music. "Unless you flew."

Zach smiled and said, "I sort of did."

Then he told her they needed to talk and couldn't do it here. Just like that Kate grabbed her book bag from underneath her seat. And they left.

When they were down the escalators and back in the lobby, Kate said, "Okay, this is as long as I'm waiting. We've got some major weirdness going on here. Did you get on that bus before or not?"

"I did," Zach said. "Walk with me and I'll try to explain."

They walked up to 34th Street and then started heading east, past Macy's and Herald Square. The words came out of Zach like a blast of air. He told her about how strange he'd been feeling lately, like someone else had been living inside him. He told her about the cab dropping him off by Land's End. Then he told her about the old man, this stranger who seemed to know everything about his dad and him. And how he was certain that the man knew even more, including about the crash.

He told her what Mr. Herbert had said about the magic.

"Magic?" she said. "Like pulling a rabbit out of your hat or a quarter out from behind your ear?"

"Not exactly."

"Then what exactly?"

They were already to Fifth Avenue by now, ready for the long, straight shot up to the apartment.

"You said I could tell it my way," Zach said, and he had been, trying to tell it in some kind of order, as it had all happened, knowing the whole time he was saving the best stuff for last.

"Okay, I'll shut up," Kate said.

"See, when I said that I flew here, I wasn't lying. Only I didn't take a plane or a helicopter. I started running after the old man and the next thing I knew, well, I was back here."

"You ran all the way from the Hamptons to New York City? Please tell me you're not making this all up," Kate said. "That you didn't hop off the Jitney at the airport stop and take a cab back to the city just to game me."

Zach told her the truth. "Not my brand."

She stared hard at him, then said, "I know."

Neither one of them moving.

"Powers," Kate said.

"Yeah."

"Well, *that's* a little unexpected."

"You think?"

She smiled then, not the way she did when she was making fun of him. Just a smile that told Zach that she believed him.

It was the kind of smile that made him feel as if everything was going to be all right, even though he knew that probably wasn't true, that nothing was going to be the same for him ever again.

"I guess that leaves me with only one question," Kate said.

"Shoot."

Kate Paredes smiled at him again and said, "Are you gonna have to wear a cape?"

WHAT did his mom know about all this?

Mr. Herbert had said he was a friend of the family. If that was the truth, and who knew *what* the truth was with this guy, did that just mean Zach's dad?

Or did it mean his mom was in on the secret, too?

But if he asked her about Mr. Herbert, he'd have to explain how he'd met the old man. Every time Zach played it out in his head, no matter how many different ways he tried to start the conversation, it didn't end well for him.

Forget about superpowers. Zach didn't think he had the *brain*power to carry it off. He still had to find a way, not just to ask his mom about the old man, but about what the old man had *said*.

Had his dad really had powers? And if so, why hadn't they saved his life?

Zach waited until the next morning. He and his mom were having their Sunday morning breakfast at their favorite coffee shop. They had been coming here every Sunday for years, always taking the same back booth. Zach always ordered what his dad used to call his "truck stop breakfast": scrambled eggs and ham with a small stack of pancakes on the side and home fries. He was even allowed to have a black-and-white milk shake.

Today he was polishing off the last of his home fries when he said, "Mom, is there anything about Dad that I don't know that I should?"

As casual as if he'd asked her to pass the salt.

She was wearing a Harvard sweatshirt that had belonged to his dad. It looked huge on her, yet she never seemed to care. She wore it every Sunday, like it was her coffee-shop uniform.

She smiled at Zach over her coffee cup.

"There's a question out of left field."

Zach wanted to keep it light. "You ever wonder why it's not right field, or center?"

"No," she said. "I never did. But this isn't a baseball conversation, is it?"

He shook his head. "Dad," he said.

She put her cup down and leaned forward. "Well," she

said, "I think there was a lot *I* didn't know about your dad's work."

"I'm not asking about his work," Zach said. "I know a lot of that was classified or top secret and all that. And that he was never really telling us everything, even when one of his missions was over. That's not what I'm talking about. I was wondering if there was stuff I ought to know about, like, his *life.*"

It wasn't the first time Zach had wondered about this. Even when his dad was alive, Zach had never learned as much about Tom Harriman's early life as he wanted to. He knew that his dad had been an orphan, raised in group homes until he finally got foster parents—Richard and Carol Harriman—about the time he was Zach's age.

Richard and Carol had been in their fifties at the time and living in Greenwich, Connecticut. They paid for Tom to go to Brunswick Academy, a fancy private school, and saw him become a three-sport star there and president of the student body before he went off to Harvard.

The Harrimans died his freshman year at Harvard, in a car accident.

"They gave me a life," he'd said to Zach once. "I just wish they could have seen how it turned out."

Zach had heard plenty about his dad's high school years, and his college years, but very little about being an orphan, the group homes, about growing up without parents. Tom Harriman had never said anything about trying to find out who his birth parents were.

Zach had asked his dad once what he'd been like as a kid. Tom Harriman just smiled and said, "Exactly like I am now, just younger."

Zach had always wanted more. Now he *needed* more.

He asked his mom, "Did he ever tell you about when he was young?"

"No," she said. "Usually he'd just make a joke out of it. If I tried to press him, and I *did* try to press him occasionally, he'd just say, 'Oh, sure, beat up on the orphan boy.' But then he *always* used humor when he wanted to keep me at arm's length. If we'd have one of our rare arguments and he knew he was in trouble, he'd say, 'You can't make me go live on the street. Been there, done that.' I know there had to have been some terrible times for him, but I couldn't ever press him enough to get him to talk about them. Now I wish I had."

"Me too."

The coffee shop was emptier than usual today, quieter, so Zach tried to keep his voice low. "Did he have any *talents* he never talked to me about?"

"You mean like sports talents? Come on, you know what he was like. As far as I could tell, he could do anything he wanted to. And well. From rock climbing to high diving to running marathons. He was almost like a freak when it came to all that."

Freak, Zach thought.

With a freak boy. Who knew Spence's nickname for him would be so dead-on?

"And in addition to everything else," Elizabeth Harriman said, "he thought he was the greatest pilot on the planet." She put sad eyes on Zach and said, "Sorry, kiddo."

"No need to apologize."

If she was holding back, keeping something from him, she was doing a world-class job of it.

But he stayed with it.

"Nothing out of the ordinary, though?"

"Where are we going with this, pal?"

"I'm just curious," he said. "Didn't you always tell me curious was a good thing? You know what they used to say about Dad: there had to be three Tom Harrimans to accomplish everything he accomplished in his life."

"I'm just curious about where the curiosity is coming from *today*?" his mom said.

"I'm just like you, Mom. I never pressed him enough when I had the chance. So now I'm pressing *you*."

"I'll answer you this way," she said. "I guess I never

thought he was doing anything out of the ordinary because he was so *extra*ordinary at everything."

One last shot, like he was heaving a half-court shot before the horn sounded.

"No magic?" he said.

It made his mom laugh.

"Magic? Your dad couldn't even do a decent card trick."

Over the next few days he was barely able to focus on school or basketball or anything. All he could think about was what had happened in that field.

The field where his dad's plane had crashed had changed everything for him. *Twice.*

Zach went through the motions in his classes and with his homework. He and Kate even pulled off an A on the Addison-FDR project. And he managed not to suck in basketball, shooting the ball a little better and playing some decent defense. Maybe because he wasn't trying so hard, or maybe because it didn't matter as much as it had when practice had started.

He was even managing to stay off Spence Warren's smack list. Both physical and mental. His father had told him once that bullies the world over had one thing in common: they hated people standing up to them. Maybe that's what finally got Spence off his back—that fight in the park, even though Zach hadn't given him much of a fight.

At least he'd *felt* like fighting. Finally fighting back.

No matter where he was or what he was doing, though, he kept waiting for that *feeling* to come over him again, the crazy one that had him thinking he was about to turn into a werewolf.

Waiting and wondering what would happen to him the next time.

Could he fly? Make himself invisible again? Could he take Spence Warren in a fair fight? Could he turn these powers, whatever they were, on and off, as easily as if he were putting his laptop to sleep?

Yet nothing new happened. Just the regulation Zach Harriman. No old wizards jumping out of the weeds like grasshoppers. No weird trips into the park at night. No urge to pick a fight with a wall, or with Spence, or scare off muggers hiding in the bushes.

"I feel like I'm in an elevator," he said to Kate. A full week had now passed between meeting Mr. Herbert and today. They were walking home from a movie. "Stuck between floors. Not even knowing if I'm going up or down."

She giggled. "Sounds like your normal state, if you ask me."

"That's supposed to be helpful?"

"Not to you, maybe. But it makes me happy."

"Seriously," he said, "does this make any sense to you?"

"Seriously? Yeah, I get it. You feel like your life went to a commercial break and you're waiting for the show to come back on. Only it won't. This whole week . . . you haven't been able to do anything like you did getting home from Montauk? Anything out of, like, *Smallville*, Superboy?"

Zach shook his head. "The only thing out of the ordinary was staying awake for a whole science class."

"My God, man, you *are* superhuman!"

"Do you think I should head out to that field again?"

"Not really. I mean, if this really is your life now, then it's going to happen wherever you are. Right?"

Zach nodded.

They had entered Central Park by now and were walking around the reservoir. It was starting to get dark, and the temperature had dropped about ten degrees since they'd left the movie theater.

"Sometimes I think I imagined the whole thing."

"But that would mean I imagined it, too," Kate said. "That would be some hallucination, Harriman. Two for the price of one."

Zach casually reached into his pocket, felt for his

dad's Morgan. He kept it with him all the time, except when he was at basketball practice.

It felt warm, the way it had in Montauk.

Not good, Zach thought.

Not good at all.

ZACH could swear there had been plenty of joggers in the park only a moment before. Some of them had even passed him and Kate. Yet now he couldn't see any of them as they came around to the west side of the reservoir. It was as if somebody had waved them off the running track all at once.

Now it was just Zach and Kate.

And the three guys blocking their way.

Zach and Kate stopped. Instinctively, Kate reached for his hand. There was no mistaking what was about to happen with the three guys.

Trouble.

Two of them casually moved behind Zach and Kate.

The one in front said to Zach, "Empty your pockets."

Zach said, "I know you."

He was sure he did, sure that the face underneath the black knit cap was the same one he'd seen the other night in the park.

Staring at him now, Zach said, "You were going to jump that woman that night, weren't you?"

Kate said, "What night?"

Zach ignored her. "I'm right, aren't I?" he said to Knit Cap.

"Shut up, kid," the guy said.

"All I've got in my pocket is about four dollars and change," Zach said.

"I don't want the four dollars, and I don't want the chump change," he said. "I want the coin."

"The Morgan? How do you know . . . ?"

The guy looked at his two buddies and said, "I told you. Kid's clueless."

"Well, I know *I* am," Kate said, trying to sound normal, Zach knowing better, hearing the change in her voice.

Hearing how scared she was.

"I know this," Zach said. "My dad gave me this coin and there's no way I'm handing it over to some scrub like you."

And just like that, he started to feel it.

Not the fear he knew Kate was feeling.

The other feeling.

A roar inside his head. Inside *him*.

"Zach?" Kate said.

"It's okay, Kate."

"Don't," she said in a small voice. "Just give them what they want and let's get out of here."

He turned to her, smiling now, actually enjoying himself. "See, their problem is, they don't know how badly I've got them outnumbered."

A lot happened then, seemingly all at once.

Someone reached for Kate's arms, but she wheeled and dove away from him, off the track and onto the grass, rolling as she landed.

Leaving Zach and the three men.

Not really knowing how to do what he wanted to do, Zach wheeled and hit the guy who had reached for Kate with an elbow that caught him cleanly on the jaw. Direct hit. Zach heard a sound that reminded him of the crack of a bat in baseball. The guy staggered back but didn't go down, gave his head a quick shake and started to raise his fists.

Too late.

Without even feeling himself make the move, Zach was behind him, reaching up, putting his hand on the guy's neck, knowing exactly what to do, finding the pressure point like it had an X drawn on it. He squeezed hard and put him out.

One against two now.

The odds getting worse for them by the minute.

He was about to go for Knit Cap when he heard Kate yell, "Watch out!" Out of the corner of his eye he saw the other guy, the widest of the three, circling to the right, holding a metal pipe in his hand.

Zach covered the distance between them with the kind of blinding first step he wished he had in hoops. He took the pipe out of the guy's hand like he was taking a pacifier away from a baby.

Then Zach drop-stepped away, giving himself just enough room to jump and spin and take him down with the kind of move that would have made Jackie Chan proud.

Now it was just him and Knit Cap.

Zach was anxious to finish this, knowing it had started that night when Knit Cap was in the bushes, waiting for the woman jogger.

Zach dropped the metal pipe at his feet. He didn't need it.

"How did you know about the coin?" Zach said, taking a step forward.

Knit Cap shook his head.

"Not today, kid. Maybe another time. But not today."

Then instead of moving on Zach, he turned and ran in the other direction, went up and over the tall iron fence in one move, like someone in a highlight reel slam dunk, and dove into the water of the reservoir.

Zach ran to the fence, waiting to see the guy come up.

Only he didn't. The water was completely still, without even the kind of ripple you got when you threw a stone into it.

He waited for what felt like a long time and then walked back to the track. Confused.

Kate was on her knees in the grass, staring at him.

"Zach?" she said in a quiet voice, his name like a question to her.

Zach said, "The other two . . . they ran off?"

Kate shook her head. Somehow Zach had known she would.

"No," she said. Her voice wasn't much more than a whisper.

"Where are they then?"

"They disappeared," she said.

Her eyes were wide, frightened.

"Like they were . . . deleted," she said.

KATE Paredes considered herself a brave girl.

She didn't wander *all* over the city by herself, but neither was she easily intimidated by it. Her mother, her wonderful mother, Alba, the giver of the best advice in two languages, had once told her something she never forgot:

"If you think you're in the wrong place, you probably are."

Kate didn't take silly chances, but that didn't mean she didn't like to test herself occasionally. Get out of her comfort zone. The summer before, despite all the kidding she got from Zach, she'd signed up for Outward Bound, putting herself out there in the woods of Maine for a couple of weeks. And she'd liked that more than she thought she would, relying on herself, being strong and resourceful and using common sense.

From the start, she'd understood that when it came to her and Zach, she was the stronger one. It wasn't as though she thought he was some kind of wimp. Just that if one of them was going to lean on the other, Zach was going to be the leaner.

Not anymore.

Not after what she'd seen today, with her own eyes. This wasn't Zach telling her about the old man, about the way he'd gotten back to the city.

This time it was right in front of her.

The Zach she'd seen at the reservoir, the Zach she'd seen take down two men . . . she didn't know that Zach Harriman.

Spins and kicks and jumps and . . . *fearlessness*. The weird calm, the confident way he took on those guys. Like he *knew* he could take them.

This Zach had scared the brave girl.

He scared her and so did this new world of his, the one with the magic in it, with bad guys who disappeared into thin air, with danger, and Kate somehow knew this wasn't going to be the last violence in it.

Kate lay in the dark that night and kept replaying what had happened, a much scarier version of counting sheep. And even when she finally fell asleep, there were nightmares that she would still remember, much too vividly, in the morning.

Nightmares about men disappearing every time she tried to get a good look at them. And about someone she felt should be a friend, but who had the face of a stranger.

She woke up early on Sunday morning, happy not to be sleeping anymore. She was up before her mother, something that hardly ever happened, and felt like the first person awake in the whole city of New York.

She felt trapped in her room, time moving way too slowly. She needed a way to breathe again. So even though it was a few minutes before six, she decided to get dressed and go out for a walk. Maybe stop at Starbucks and buy herself a hot chocolate. Extra whipped cream.

She put on her absolute favorite ball cap, the Knicks cap that Zach had bought her, and a Parker hoodie, went down the elevator and out past Mitch, one of the weekend doormen, with a big smile and wave.

"I'd say top of the mornin', missy, but it's more like the bottom of the night," Mitch said. "Where you off to?"

"I want to be the first person in Manhattan to get a hot chocolate at Starbucks today," she said.

"Ah yes, the breakfast of champions."

"Maybe the Knicks should try some," Kate said. "With extra whipped cream."

"Sometimes they're about as tough as whipped cream," Mitch said.

"'Cept for David Lee."

Mitch winked at her. "'Cept for him. Think they'll let him go?"

"They better not."

She walked north on Fifth Avenue for a while and then cut over to Madison and what she knew would be the first Starbucks she'd come to. Went big today—a venti.

The hot chocolate felt comforting, the large cup solid and warm in her hands. After a few sips she left and, instead of heading back home, she walked to Fifth Avenue and turned north again. The wall to Central Park was on her left.

She told herself she hadn't planned to end up here. Yet Kate knew she was kidding herself. She knew exactly what her destination was from the moment she'd left her bedroom. She was walking back up to the reservoir, back to where it had happened. Maybe just to see some sign that it had all been real, that it hadn't been part of one long nightmare.

She cut into the park past the Metropolitan Museum of Art and made her way up some steps to the running track. The sun still wasn't up yet, but there were already a few stray joggers.

She finished her hot chocolate and dropped the cup in a waste bin, all the while waiting for her cell to ring, waiting for her mother to be calling.

Silence.

She walked until she got to the old brick maintenance building. She looked behind her and could see only one jogger, all the way at the far end of the water, coming up the same stairs she had just climbed a few minutes before.

Kate stopped, making sure she was in the right spot. She knelt in the grass, getting up and making a wider circle, thinking that maybe the metal pipe the one guy had been carrying would be around here somewhere.

Something she could put her hands on.

Nothing.

Somehow she knew there wouldn't be.

A voice in her head told her to leave, that this was all bigger than her.

Kate ignored it.

She closed her eyes and saw it all happening again, pictured the guy in the knit cap going over the fence as easily as if he were hopping a footstool and then disappearing into the water, not making a ripple or a sound.

She had watched him do it. When she turned back around, the other two men had vanished. Could they have just run toward Central Park West while she wasn't looking instead of disappearing completely?

No.

"You came back. I knew you would."

In the quiet of the morning, the emptiness of this part of the park, it was as if the words came out of a loudspeaker.

Kate screamed, couldn't help it, whipped her head around.

Knit Cap, dressed exactly the same.

Kate opened her mouth again, ready to scream for help . . . only this time nothing came out.

He smiled at her. But this wasn't a friendly smile; there was nothing good behind his eyes, nothing good inside him at all.

"But what *was* she thinking?" he said, circling her. "I mean, coming back here all alone?"

"Stay away from me," Kate said, knowing as soon as she did how pathetic that sounded.

She added: "What do you want from me?"

"From you?" he said. "Nothing. I want your boy-friend."

"He's not my boyfriend," Kate said.

Even here, even like this, there was something that made her want to set the record straight.

"Right."

"Why don't you just swim away like you did the last time and leave me alone?"

The brave girl trying one last time to sound brave, even if she wasn't.

"No, I don't think so," he said, stopping in front of her, leaning down, his face only inches from hers. "I think I have other plans."

She tried to look past him, down the track, wondering where the jogger had gone.

"There's no one around to help you," he said. "Look around all you want."

"I'm going now," Kate said, trying to make her voice sound steady.

He reached for her.

KATE tried to duck away. No good. The man just grabbed the back of her hoodie.

She tried to scream. Same as before: nothing came out. Knit Cap pulled harder on the hoodie, spun her around toward him.

That's when Kate saw the jogger reappear around the corner.

Only he wasn't jogging. You couldn't even call this running. He was moving way too fast.

Kate tried to look away, didn't want Knit Cap to see her staring, didn't want him to know they were no longer alone. Knowing there was only one person this could be.

. . .

Zach hadn't told Kate about *all* of his new powers, mainly because he was still figuring them out.

One thing he had definitely noticed, though: his senses had suddenly been jacked up.

Jacked up a lot.

His eyesight, which had always been solid when he was reading an eye chart, was *off* the charts now, sharper than hi-def. He was sure that was why his jump shot was suddenly better than ever in basketball.

But this morning it had been his hearing that had gotten him going. Zach had heard Kate on the stairs, even though she had done an expert job of sneaking down. He'd also heard the elevator opening and closing, as though the door were right next to his bed.

He saw the time in the glowing numbers of his clock radio and wondered where she could be going at six a.m. He didn't like it.

He went to the balcony and saw her with Mitch the doorman.

Saw her head up Fifth Avenue.

Zach didn't wait. He threw on his jeans and fleece jacket and sneaks, not even waiting for the elevator, taking the back stairs and taking them fast.

He followed Kate at a distance, wondering where the

girl who could sleep until noon if you let her was going to so early. He figured the mystery was solved when she went into Starbucks and emerged a few minutes later with a giant cup of what he knew had to be hot chocolate. He waited for her to turn back home.

Only, she didn't.

And now Zach wondered if he was developing a sixth sense. Because he knew exactly where she was going.

Like she was the one who needed to test herself in the park, the way he had.

He stayed a block behind and out of sight, watched her cut into the park past the Met, watched her go up the steps and take a left, walking toward the maintenance building. Zach kept his eyes on her, was ready to dart off the path a couple of times when she'd stopped and looked behind her. She almost caught him once, so he started jogging in the other direction.

When he looked back, he saw that Kate was no longer alone.

And even from a couple of hundred yards away, Zach could see who was with her on the track.

He saw the guy pulling Kate by her hood and was sure he could hear her silent scream.

And Zach Harriman was on the move.

KNIT Cap never even saw Zach coming.

Zach grabbed him from behind with a fistful of his black windbreaker.

Before he had a chance to lay a hand on Kate.

Kate watched Zach the way someone watches fireworks on the Fourth of July.

Zach couldn't believe that Knit Cap had come back here, that he was enough of an idiot to think he could get away with messing with Kate.

His problem, not mine, Zach thought.

He lifted Knit Cap off the ground, a little surprised at how easy it was, how light the guy felt to him. Then Zach launched him through the air in almost the same motion, like the guys picking up trash in front of his building tossed bags into the back of the truck.

Knit Cap landed hard in the grass.

Sweet.

"Stay out of the way," Zach said to Kate.

"Nice to see you, too," she said.

The guy tried to roll up into a sitting position, trying to get up, to fight back. He couldn't.

"Enough," he said.

"That's my line," Zach said. "You come near her again, even *think* about putting your hands near her again, it will be much worse."

Zach knelt down in front of him now. He grabbed the front of his jacket, pulled him close and said, "Why are you doing this?"

Knit Cap was breathing hard, no expression on his face, eyes on Zach.

"I *said*, why do you keep doing this? What do you want from me?"

Nothing.

Zach shouted at him now. *"Who sent you?"*

Knit Cap finally spoke. "You're not asking the right questions, kid. At least your father asked the right questions."

Zach shook the guy now, snapping his head back.

"What do you know about my father?"

"A lot, Zacman," he said, finishing with the type of smug grin Zach was used to seeing from Spence.

Zach felt like he'd been punched.

Another person who knew that name.

"Now what do you say you let me go?"

"Not until you tell me what I want to know," Zach said.

Knit Cap grinned again. "You *are* like him in one way, I have to say that. Neither of you knows what he doesn't know. Or, in his case, didn't know."

Zach pictured himself knocking the smile off the guy's face. Forced himself to breathe before he spoke.

"Again," he said, "what do you know about my father?"

"Like I said—a lot. But I'm not the one to tell you, kid, no matter how much you bounce me around."

And in that moment, Zach knew the guy was telling him the truth, at least about that.

He gave him one more shove, unclenched his fists— when was the last time they *hadn't* been clenched?— and let him go.

Zach stood up first.

The guy's grin was back.

"You gotta chill, Zacman."

"Don't! Don't call me that."

"See, that's what I'm talking about. Even on that

you gotta chill. You did good today. Better than I expected."

Then he stood, turned and ran down the track. In a matter of seconds he was gone again, disappeared.

Kate was standing next to Zach now.

"You let him go," she said.

"He'll be back," Zach answered.

"That's what I'm afraid of."

AS winter made the turn toward spring in New York City, Zach's mom began to spend more time with Uncle John.

Zach kept finding out more and more about his new self, testing the range of his powers whenever he could. As he did so, he saw his mom finally turning into her old self.

First it was dinner out at a restaurant. Then a Broadway show opening. Then there was a trip to the movies, over on 86th Street, which turned into a weekly event for her and Uncle John.

One time they were coming in just as Zach was preparing to sneak past the night doorman again and patrol the city for a couple of hours, and he'd had to scramble back into his bed.

Finally, one night, his mom downstairs waiting for Uncle John to pick her up, Zach used the *D* word on her.

"What time is your date?" he asked.

She laughed, but in the high-pitched way she did when she was nervous or embarrassed.

"A *date*? With John Marshall? Stop your crazy talk."

He grinned, letting her know he was playing. "Okay, if it's not a date, what would you call it?"

"It's dinner, mister. With maybe some coffee afterward."

"Well, then, I guess what I'm really asking here is the difference between a date with somebody and going out to dinner, including coffee afterward, with the same somebody."

"It's been too long since my last date—with your father, I might add—for me to even *remember* dating. This is dinner. With your Uncle John."

They were on the long couch in the living room.

"Hey," she said. "This isn't bothering you, is it? Me getting out of the house a little for something other than the campaign?"

"Nope."

"You sure?"

"Yup."

"Your Uncle John isn't just a good friend. He's practically family."

"Mom, you think I don't know that?"

"He was like a brother to your father."

"A band of brothers, Dad always said. Even though there were only two guys in the band."

She slid down the couch, put an arm around him, kissed him on top of his head.

"I know you were just kidding," she said. "But the thing you were kidding about? It's not like that between John and me. Not now, not ever. Not happening."

Zach wondered if Uncle John would have answered the same way.

And his mom, being a mom, must have mentioned their conversation to Uncle John, because the next Saturday morning when Zach came down for breakfast, Uncle John was sitting in the kitchen waiting for him.

He was in jeans, sneakers and his favorite Red Sox sweatshirt. It had always been a fun competition between Zach's dad and Uncle John. Tom Harriman bled the dark blue of Yankee pinstripes. Uncle John had grown up outside of Boston and was a Red Sox fan. It was probably the only thing they'd ever disagreed on.

"Get dressed," Uncle John said. "We're going to do something we haven't done in way too long."

"What?"

"Young Zachary, you and I are going to have ourselves a good old-fashioned knock-around day."

Zach rubbed the sleep out of his eyes. "With you wearing a Red Sox sweatshirt around New York? Yeah, we're gonna get knocked around all right."

"Talk, talk, talk. More dressing, less talking. Adventures await."

Zach's first knock-around day with Uncle John was four years ago, when Uncle John saw how much Zach had been missing his dad. Over the years they'd kept up the tradition—always when Zach's dad was away. The rules were simple: Zach could go anywhere in the city he wanted, sometimes three or four stops before they were through. But he could only pick out one at a time. No itinerary. No game plan. They would just make up a Saturday or Sunday as they went along. Sometimes they'd have a car and a driver, sometimes they'd take cabs, sometimes they'd use the subway.

Always, though, it was big bangin' fun.

They ate a *lot* of junk food, usually every few hours whether they were hungry or not. Uncle John insisted that knock-around days, if done right, should resemble all-you-can-eat contests.

Since it was already eleven-thirty by the time Zach got dressed and came back downstairs, he announced that he was going to skip breakfast and go straight to lunch.

"Where?" Uncle John said. They had a car waiting for them downstairs.

"Sylvia's," Zach said.

The best and most famous restaurant in Harlem. Serving the best food, at least in Zach's estimation, in the whole city.

"Done."

They ate like complete idiots, Zach ordering the meat loaf smothered in Sylvia's "secret sauce," with garlic mashed potatoes and ribs on the side, followed by coconut cake for dessert.

"You go wherever you want to next," Uncle John said. "Just drop me off at the emergency room."

"You're the one who says we have to pig out."

"I didn't know Sylvia was going to bat leadoff."

"Speaking of which," Zach said, "I *have* picked where I want to go next."

"Say the word."

"Two words: Citi Field. To get us ready for the baseball season." Zach shrugged. "Unless you can't get us in, of course."

Uncle John already had his cell phone out. "Can I get us *in*? Is the pope Catholic? Did the Knicks stink last night?"

"Ouch."

Uncle John walked a few feet down the sidewalk on

Lenox Avenue, came back two minutes later and said, "We're in. I hope that didn't take too long."

He winked at Zach.

A half hour later they were standing in the outfield under the huge old-fashioned Pepsi sign.

"I still don't understand how you became a Mets fan," Uncle John said.

"Simple: David Wright." Then he said, "Am I allowed to run the bases?"

"Knock yourself out."

Zach stood in the batter's box, which had already been drawn in brilliant white, even though opening day was still a few weeks away. Then he took off for first, took off for real, running the bases hard, touching the inside corner of each base like his dad had taught him.

Fifteen feet from home plate, he launched into a head-first slide, not worrying about getting dirty, not on a knock-around day. He slid around an imaginary tag, reaching back to touch the plate with an outstretched hand.

"I thought the catcher might have nicked you on the way by," Uncle John said.

"Nope. Never touched me."

"First run of the season," Uncle John said. "Your old man would have been proud."

As soon as he'd brought up Zach's dad, Zach could see from the look on his face he was sorry he had.

"Don't worry, Uncle J.," Zach said. "I miss him all the time, whether we're talking about him or not."

"Me too."

They walked through the Mets dugout. One of the security guards let Zach have a look inside the clubhouse, which was filled with unpacked boxes waiting for the season. When they were outside in the parking lot, Uncle John said, "There's a method to my madness today, by the way."

Zach nodded. "Figured."

"I don't want you to have the wrong idea about your mom and me."

"I don't."

"Yeah," Uncle John said, "I think you do. And I would, too. There's a line your old man liked to use, from an old joke: 'It's not so funny when it's *your* mom.' So I get it, young Zachary. I really do."

"So do I," Zach said. "Really, I do."

"But whether you do or not, I want you to understand. I always told your dad that I'd look after both of you if anything ever happened to him. And that's what I'm doing. Trying to keep a promise to your dad. Not trying to *be* your dad. Okay?"

"Okay."

Uncle John put out his fist. Zach pounded it lightly.

"Pact?" Uncle John said.

"Pact."

"Now let's blow this pop stand."

"'Blow this pop stand'? Wow. You're older than I thought."

"Oh," Uncle John said, "you have no idea."

They ate cheeseburgers at P. J. Clarke's on Third Avenue when they got back to Manhattan, Zach polishing *them* off with apple pie and ice cream. As he did, he noticed Uncle John staring at him, shaking his head.

"What?"

"Your old man ate like this. Always. Starting in college. Never gained a stinking pound." He winked. "You remind me more of him all the time."

Zach kept shoveling in the pie and ice cream, thinking that Uncle John didn't know the half of it.

It was late afternoon by the time they walked out of Clarke's, but Zach still wasn't ready to go home.

Neither was Uncle John, apparently. "Where to next?" he said.

"We walk."

"Where?"

"My favorite place in the city," Zach said. *"Anywhere."*

Anywhere turned out to be Central Park. Even on a knock-around day he felt himself being drawn there.

They gradually made their way east and north, passed by horse-drawn hansom cabs and bikers and joggers. The more they walked, the less they spoke, not because they'd run out of things to say, just because the quiet seemed to fit them right now, both of them letting the last of the afternoon just *be*.

They were past the zoo, heading toward the 66th Street entrance, when Zach said, "Thanks, Uncle John. I'm done."

Uncle John laughed. "Oh, you don't know how happy I am to hear you say that, Zachary. Because old Uncle John was done at about 59th and Third."

"I thought I saw a look when the last hansom cab went past us," Zach said. "Like you wanted to kick out that nice couple and jump in."

"You know me *so* well," Uncle John said as he laughed.

Then he wasn't laughing, or walking. He'd stopped the same as Zach had.

Both of them staring at the giant.

HE was the biggest person Zach had ever seen outside of an NBA game, dressed in a dark suit and old-fashioned brim hat pulled low over his eyes. His features were distorted, almost like he was wearing a mask. His hands alone were the size of basketballs.

There was no way for Zach to be sure what seven feet tall looked like in street clothes. But if this guy wasn't all of that, he was close, and looked as if he weighed enough to shove Shaq out of the paint.

Zach looked around. Nobody else in sight. Like somehow the stage had been emptied for him again.

The man said to Uncle John, "The boy is coming with me."

Uncle John stepped forward, trying to protect Zach. "I don't know who you are or what you're talking about. But this boy isn't going anywhere with you."

"I'm not leaving without him. I'm not like the others."

"What others?"

"Ask the boy."

"Zach," Uncle John said, eyes not leaving the giant. "Do you know this man?"

"No."

The giant said, "No games this time."

"*What* games?" Uncle John said. Standing his ground. Head tilted back like he was looking up at a tall building.

"Leave us. Now."

Then Uncle John shouted, "Run, Zach!" as he ducked and charged forward, driving a shoulder into the giant's stomach.

The huge man didn't flinch, or move, or even acknowledge that he'd been hit. He just shook his head, almost in disgust, grabbed Uncle John by the shoulders, lifted him as easily as he would a toy and threw him in an arc across the open field to his left.

In that moment John Marshall looked as if he'd been

shot out of an invisible cannon, flying, before he landed at the base of a thick old tree with a truly sickening thud.

Then he lay still.

The giant reached for Zach, saying, "Let's go."

And without planning it, without even thinking about it, just on fire again, Zach Harriman was the one in the air.

He was the one flying.

He elevated like LeBron and then just hung there in midair in front of the giant, scissor-kicking him in the middle of his face.

"Yeah," Zach said. "Let's go."

Still in the air.

Not for long.

Unlike Knit Cap, the giant fought back. He backhanded Zach out of the air like King Kong swatting airplanes. This time it was Zach hitting the ground hard.

In pain, a lot of pain, but trying to roll away.

He felt a huge hand on him then, felt himself being turned around as though he weighed nothing. There was blood on the giant's face where Zach had connected with his nose.

"Don't get ahead of yourself," the giant said. "You're not ready yet for someone like me."

Then came these giant hands again, catching Zach on the side of his head. Zach went down.

The giant kicked him. Zach heard shouts, a siren slowly getting louder.

Then he didn't hear anything.

ZACH wasn't sure what day it was.

Or whether he was awake or asleep. He just knew that sleep seemed much, *much* better right now, because sleep meant he wouldn't be hurting nearly as much.

He was in New York Hospital, in a room overlooking the East River, in a wing named after his mom's father. When he managed to open his eyes, which wasn't often, he saw his mom. Kate was there a couple of times, too. And Uncle John. But he was never awake long before a doctor or nurse entered the room, took his temperature, gave him a pill to swallow, checked his eyes and told him to go back to sleep.

Even talking hurt, though one time Zach had said to his mom in a weak voice, "You should see the other guy."

"I'm just grateful to see *you*," she'd said. "You had a concussion, though what you're feeling the most is two broken ribs. The doctors say those are going to hurt for a month or so, maybe more, no matter what they do for them." His mom put a cool hand on Zach's forehead and said, "Other than that, no permanent damage to my boy."

Zach had closed his eyes again and let whatever medicine they were giving him take him until he was back to sleep again. He dreamed of his dad more than once, kept seeing his lips moving, knew that his dad was trying to tell him something, but he couldn't make out the words.

The dreams felt so real.

The next time Zach woke up, in the night, Dr. Vann was there.

"So how we doing?" Dr. Vann asked.

"A little less rap music inside my head."

"Excellent." He shined his small flashlight into Zach's eyes, took his temperature again. "You're a remarkably fast healer, my friend. Speaking of friends, I said your good-byes for the night to both friends and family. Miss Kate, by the way, thought she was getting ready to sleep on the floor next to your bed. I told her you'd be fine on your own."

"And she listened to you?" Zach said. "Doc, you're not just a healer. You're a miracle worker."

"Maybe I am. Now go to sleep."

"I'm wide awake."

Dr. Vann said, "Not for long."

Zach closed his eyes. Maybe he would dream of his dad again.

"Zacman."

It had to be a dream, had to be his dad talking to him. So at first he was afraid to open his eyes, afraid the dream would leave him, the way the good ones sometimes did right before you woke up in the morning.

"Zacman. I know you can hear me. Open your eyes."

He turned toward the voice, groaning as he did, feeling the stab of his ribs.

He opened his eyes now in the half-light of the hospital room and saw that it wasn't his dad talking.

It was Mr. Herbert.

He looked the same as he had out at Land's End. Same jacket. Same old jeans. Same white hair.

Zach said, "How'd you get in here?"

The old man grinned. "You've got your ways of getting where you need to, I have mine."

"I ran out of magic," Zach said.

Mr. Herbert shook his head. "You've got all the magic

you need, boy. More than you know and as much as your father. Yet let this be a lesson—you're only fourteen. And you're still human."

"Had to be a better way for me to learn that."

"No," said Mr. Herbert, "this was *exactly* the kind of lesson you needed to learn to keep living. There's a reason for everything, boy."

"My head hurts too much to play this game," Zach said. "What time is it, anyway?"

"'Bout four."

"And you just walked past everybody and got in here?"

"Told you," Mr. Herbert said. "I've still got a few tricks up my sleeve."

"So you've got your own talents, too?"

"You're the talent, boy. I'm more like your agent."

"How lucky for me," Zach said with a roll of his eyes, "you choosing me like this."

"We don't get to do the choosing, either one of us. Everything with a reason, everything with a purpose. But things are starting to speed up, which means you're going to have to pick up the pace."

Zach pictured himself reaching over and pushing his call button for a nurse, wondered if this strange man would simply disappear if somebody walked in on them.

But he didn't reach. He was interested in what the man had to say.

"I kind of . . . facilitate things. I did it with your father when I found him on the street, and now I'm doing it with you."

"What do you mean, when you found my dad on the street?" Zach said. "He never told me anything about that."

"He was about your age," Mr. Herbert said. "But let's not get ahead of ourselves. That's another story for another time."

Now Zach made himself sit up, not caring how much it made his ribs scream.

"Another person worried that I might get ahead of myself?" Zach said.

"Lower your voice," the old man said.

"The reason I'm lying here like Humpty Dumpty is because I'm *already* ahead of myself."

"You're still way ahead of where I thought you'd be, and that's a compliment."

"Pardon me if I don't thank you."

"No thanks necessary, really. The big thing now is getting you better. And I'm not talking about your health, boy. I mean we've got to get you better at being *you.*"

The old man pushed his chair back, stood up.

"You're not going anywhere," Zach said, though they both knew he couldn't do anything to stop him.

Mr. Herbert surprised him and sat back down. "You know," he said, "there's times, a look on your face, when I see the boy your father was. Or maybe it's the man you're going to become."

Zach's head was starting to throb again, more because of the conversation than the pills wearing off. But this was important.

"I get it by now," he said to Mr. Herbert, "I get the little games you like to play with me, talking in circles, or riddles, or whatever it is you do."

"They're not riddles if you know the answers."

"Stick it."

It made the old man laugh again. "Now you *really* sound like your father."

Zach closed his eyes. "Leave me alone," he said.

"There will be a time when I'll do that, when you'll be on your own," Mr. Herbert said. "But you're not ready for that yet."

"When was my dad ready?"

"He was older than you."

"And when he was, you told him what he was up against?"

"I did," Mr. Herbert said. "But when I first found him, when he was your age, I just told him about the life he was going to have, the wife and the son and all the rest of it. With him, there wasn't quite the . . . *urgency.* He had a little time to grow up into what he became. What he was destined to be."

The old man closed his eyes now, as if smiling at the memory of the young Tom Harriman. Then he snapped out of it.

"But like I keep trying to tell you: we don't have that kind of time, Zacman. I just stopped by to make sure you were okay. It's important you are."

He got up, picked up his chair and placed it against the wall, walked across the room and put his hand on the doorknob. He stopped and turned around.

"You're going to have to grow up fast, boy," Mr. Herbert said. "Fast as you can move now."

"And what happens if I don't?"

"Simple," Mr. Herbert said. "If you don't, then they win."

He held up a coin, what Zach knew instantly was a Morgan dollar, glowing in the dim light of the hospital room, and tossed it across the room.

Zach managed to reach up and catch it.

"Where . . . ?"

"You dropped it in the park, right after you got dropped on your head. I retrieved it for you."

"You were *there?*"

"Sleep tight, Zacman," the old man said.

Then he was gone.

ZACH closed his eyes again. But not to sleep. He needed to think.

The door opened. The sound of a man's footsteps. Zach was afraid to look.

"There he is," said a voice.

Uncle John.

"Hey," Zach said.

"Zachary."

"What time is it?"

"Little before four," Uncle John said. "Sorry to wake you. But this couldn't wait."

"Have you been at the hospital the whole time?"

"Went home for a few hours of quick shut-eye. But I had to come back."

"In the middle of the night?"

Uncle John said, "When I told your dad I'd look out for you, I understood it was going to be a full-time job." He rubbed his face. Even in the dim light, Zach could see that Uncle John hadn't bothered to shave in days.

"How're you feeling?"

"Been better," Zach said.

"I expect that you have," Uncle John said.

Zach managed a grin. "That wasn't the kind of knock-around day I had in mind."

"Really? Could have fooled me. You seemed pretty eager to take on that beast."

"No more eager than you were. No more than you seem now, sneaking in to see me at four in the morning."

"Needed to see you, Zachary. I've been worried sick."

"What about you? Last thing I remember, you had just gone up against a tree and lost. Are you okay?"

"Not my finest moment," Uncle John said. "My back wasn't too grateful, and I had a whopper of a headache for a while, but I wasn't hurt too badly."

He grabbed the same chair Mr. Herbert had used, sat down close to the bed.

"So tell me," Uncle John said, "what did he want?"

Zach was taken off guard. "What did who want?"

"We both know who I'm talking about. I saw him come in and I saw him leave."

This night just keeps getting stranger, Zach thought.

"Mr. Herbert, you mean?" Zach said.

John Marshall chuckled. "Is that what he's calling himself now?"

"You *know* him?" Zach said. "Wait . . . that's not his real name?"

"He goes by a lot of names. And yes, Zachary, I do know him. Unfortunately."

"Who is he? I mean, really?"

Uncle John leaned forward and said, "Someone to be feared."

"But he said he was a friend of Dad's, that he knows how Dad died. Maybe even why."

"He's *not* your friend," Uncle John said. "He wasn't your dad's friend, either. Believe me when I tell you: he's nobody's friend."

"He calls me Zacman. Only Dad ever called me that."

"I know." Uncle John reached over, put his hand on Zach's arm, gave it a squeeze. "He says a lot of things, and acts as if he knows more than he does, and that's just a way of getting close to you, now that he knows you have powers."

Zach's eyes grew wide. Uncle John gave his arm another squeeze. In a voice barely above a whisper he said, "I know, Zachary. I know. About you *and* your dad. I know everything about your dad's missions. He trusted me. Now I'm asking you to. Tell me what he told you."

"Mr. Herbert."

"We can keep calling him that, if you choose. There's been a lot of names over the years. A lot of battles."

"Battles?" Zach said. "Between *who*?"

"I don't mean to sound cryptic, Zachary, but the answer is between us and them."

Zach shook his head, hard. "That's the thing," he said. "That's the stupid thing. *Neither* of you makes any sense. Mr. Herbert, or whoever he is, keeps talking about me and my powers, but he never *says* anything. I'm not stupid. I can see there's some evil stuff going on. Now you talk about 'us and them,' which fits right in. Only, no one tells me who *they* are."

"The ones your dad always called 'the Bads,' Zachary," Uncle John said. "They're real. And they're going to keep coming because now they know you're special in the same way your father was."

"Yeah, I'm so special I ended up in the hospital. That giant took me down like I was a gnat. Why would they want me?"

"They know what I know, Zachary: that someday you'll be better than them. Same as your father."

"Same as my father?" Zach said.

"Yeah. Only he was a grown man battling other grown men. You're still a boy, Zachary. Don't rush this, no matter what that old man might tell you. Be the Zachary who downs cheeseburgers and runs the bases. And don't believe a word that old man says."

"Because you say so?"

It just came out of him. He was tired of being led around the ring like a pony, even if it was his Uncle John doing the leading now.

"Because," Uncle John said, "even though he wants you to think he is on your side and was on your father's side, he isn't. And never was. He's on the side of evil."

Zach squeezed his eyes shut. Us versus Them. Good versus Evil. Good versus the Bads. What he really felt like in that moment was that it was him against the world, that nobody was on his side.

He yanked his arm away from Uncle John and said, "I don't know who or what to believe anymore."

"Believe me. And in me. The way you always have."

Zach knew his voice was too loud, that he'd probably bring nurses with it.

But he didn't care.

"I want my dad back!" Zach said. Shouting now. "He'd tell me what to do!"

"So can I," Uncle John said. "After all, no one knew your dad better than me."

At that moment, Zach wished more than ever that he'd known more about his father. That it wasn't too late.

"Listen," Uncle John said, "I didn't just stop by to look in on you. I'm on my way to the airport for an early flight. Business trip. I didn't want to disappear without saying good-bye."

"When will you be back?"

"Hard to say," Uncle John answered. "As soon as I can. You be careful while I'm gone, okay? Don't go looking for any fights."

Tell that to the fights, Zach thought. *They're the ones that keep looking for me.*

ONE week later, Zach was back at school and feeling no pain. Yet questions never left his mind. Questions that had no answers.

Uncle John was still away, and now Zach's mom was about to go out of town herself, on her longest campaign trip yet for Senator Kerrigan, up and down California, helping out with fund-raisers.

As usual, she was dressed and ready to go thirty minutes before the car taking her to the airport was scheduled to show up. She had told Zach this was the time when the campaign was getting fun, two weeks on the road and then back to New York to get ready for the big speech Senator Kerrigan was scheduled to make in Central Park. It was expected to be the largest political rally ever held by a presidential candidate in New York City.

When the driver called to say he was out front, she walked over and pulled Zach into an embrace.

"I'll be back before you know it," she said.

"You don't have to worry about me, Mom. I'm fine now."

"Keep it that way."

Zach said, "This is real important to you, isn't it?"

Something crossed her face. A sad look Zach didn't understand.

"More than you know," she said. The elevator doors opened.

Two minutes later, Elizabeth Harriman was on the road.

It was a Saturday afternoon and Kate was at the movies with some girlfriends. Alba had gone grocery-shopping with a friend, another housekeeper in the building.

It was quiet in the apartment, and somehow the quiet made Zach restless, as if he needed to be outside. Not the kind of need that had sent him out into the night or to the reservoir to rescue Kate that day. He hadn't felt that need—or any of his newfound powers—since he'd gotten out of the hospital.

He kept telling himself it was because he wasn't

completely healed yet, that his body wasn't ready to go twelve rounds with the next giant who came along. And maybe that was part of it.

But Zach knew it was more. For the first time, he was afraid. Whatever the battles were that Uncle John had referred to, Zach knew one thing now: they were bigger than him.

A lot bigger.

One more time Zach wished for the power he didn't have, that no one had—the power to go back in time, to make things the way they were. He wanted to go back and tell his dad not to get on the plane, then sit down and ask him all the questions he couldn't get answers to now.

He'd trade everything for that.

Zach didn't go outside, afraid that no matter where he planned to go, he'd walk right back into Central Park and that trouble would be waiting for him again.

Instead he popped in one of his all-time favorite DVDs, *The Man in the Iron Mask,* getting lost in the adventures of the Musketeers. Zach sat in the den and watched the swordplay and got carried along by the story all over again, even knowing exactly how things were going to play out.

How they usually played out in the movies.

The good guys were going to win in the end.

• • •

When the movie ended, the quiet came back to the apartment, until he heard footsteps upstairs.

Had to be Alba. He'd had the sound up pretty good for the end of the movie and probably hadn't heard her come in.

Zach called her name, his voice sounding way too loud in the quiet.

No reply.

Was he hearing things?

Or was he just feeling anxious about everything since he'd come home from the hospital?

"Alba? Kate? You guys home?"

Nothing.

He walked into the foyer, stood perfectly still and listened. More quiet. There were times when he wanted to turn down the volume in his life, especially when the three women of the place were all talking at once during dinner. But now he wanted them all back, wanted to feel less alone, wanted to hear the sound of a voice other than his own.

Feeling like an idiot, he walked through every room of the first floor. In the dining room, he looked into a mirror, at his own reflection, and said, "Boo!"

Feeling even more like an idiot, he went upstairs to his room.

His laptop was on.

Only . . . he hadn't used it all day.

Downstairs, he heard the elevator doors opening and felt his heart pound. He froze. Then he heard Alba calling his name.

He was about to answer her when he looked back at his computer screen.

It was then that he saw the message.

Trust no one.

ZACH hadn't told Kate about Mr. Herbert coming to the hospital or about Uncle John. He hadn't told her that someone had snuck into the apartment and gotten on his computer and found yet another way to scare him.

He just wanted his mom to come home.

Somehow in a world that seemed to have gone completely haywire, her presence in the apartment made things seem a little more normal.

The day she arrived back, he charged down the stairs and threw his arms around her the way he used to when his dad would come home from a long trip.

"I missed you," he said.

"Missed you, too, pal." She pulled back, concerned. "Everything okay?"

Zach said, "Now it is."

After dinner that night, just the two of them, they went and sat on the balcony outside Zach's room.

"I need to tell you why I'm throwing myself into the Kerrigan campaign so fully," she said.

"I assumed it was because you just thought he was the best man for the job."

They were eating ice cream, looking out at the city.

"He *is* the best man," she said. "I'm convinced of that. But there's something more, and it involves your father, and you have a right to know and I should have told you before this."

Zach waited, thinking: *What now?*

More surprises.

"Senator Kerrigan asked your father to be his running mate," she said.

"Say *what?*"

"It's true," she said.

"Vice president . . . *Dad?*"

"Bob Kerrigan approached him with the idea when he first decided to run. Your father just laughed. But it was no joke to Senator Kerrigan. And somehow he managed to convince your father."

"But Dad used to say the only office he was fit to manage was his fantasy baseball team. And he always finished last."

"Senator Kerrigan didn't care. He said that this election was going to be about character and nobody—including *him*—had more character than your father. Besides, it's not like President Addison was going to stay in office forever. Your father needed to think about his future."

"And Dad . . . he really wanted to do it?"

"No, not at first. But he finally came around to thinking he was obligated to do it. He said he was getting too old to leap tall buildings in a single bound and that there had to be another way to help his country."

"Leap tall buildings in a single bound?"

"It's what they say Superman can do."

Superman. The way he'd always thought of his dad. Now more than ever.

Zach said, "What did Uncle John think?"

He could hear Uncle John's voice in his head, *No one knew your dad better than me.*

"He was a little funny about it, actually. He didn't like the idea. Your Uncle John isn't exactly the biggest Kerrigan fan. It was one of the few things those two actually disagreed about, other than baseball. Your father was nothing if not his own man, though. Once he had his mind made up, there was nothing anyone could say to make him change it."

Zach took a deep breath, let it out. "Why *didn't* you tell me this before?" he asked.

His mom turned and looked at him. "Because I thought it was one more thing that would make you sad. And I thought we had enough might-have-beens with your father already."

"But you're telling me now."

"I'm telling you now because I look at the Kerrigan campaign as unfinished business for your father. And if I'm not around much over the next few months the way I want to be, and the way you want me to be, you deserve to understand why."

"Vice President Dad," Zach said again.

"Yeah," his mom said. "And who knows, maybe down the road he even would have been President Dad."

She took his empty bowl with hers and went inside. Zach sat there, wondering about unfinished business more than ever.

IT was Zach's idea for him and Kate to spend spring break at the Harrimans' house on eastern Long Island.

His mom was away again, on the campaign trail. Uncle John had come and left again, and it occurred to Zach that he traveled even more than his dad used to. He wondered, not for the first time lately, what Uncle John actually did besides being the family lawyer—and just how much he had been involved with his dad's secret missions.

Anyway, with no one around besides Alba, Zach was eager to leave the city behind for a week. He remembered his dad telling him once that the best time to go to the beach was when you had it to yourself.

Zach, Kate and Alba took the Jitney out, Zach thinking

that the last time he had gotten on this bus, he'd ended up a whole new person with a whole new life . . . even if that life seemed to be on hold right now, like somebody's finger was on the pause button.

As soon as they were in the house, in the town between East Hampton and Montauk called Amagansett, Zach and Kate got their bikes out of the garage and rode them the half mile to the beach.

Kate had brought a blanket and snacks. They plopped down on the blanket and took off their sneakers. With the ocean in front of them, they felt as if the rest of the world were behind them. Staring at all that water made Zach feel small and normal again.

"Hey, stranger," Kate said finally.

It made him smile.

"I have gone all strange on you, haven't I?"

She said, "My general thinking is that developing superpowers will do that to a person."

"You know," he said, "I was thinking something on the way out."

"Snoring is called thinking now? Wow. Who knew?"

"Seriously," Zach said. "I was thinking that I miss the days when Spence Warren was the biggest problem in my life."

"Yeah," Kate said, high-fiving him. "Good *times!*"

She propped herself up on an elbow, turned to face him. "Did some new goon guy show up that you haven't told me about?"

"Nope. But it's not exactly as if I've been prowling around looking for any."

When he'd gotten out of the hospital, he'd admitted to her about being scared—not only of his own powers, but of whatever powers were out there lining up against him.

"You can handle anything anybody throws at you," Kate said. "With my help, of course."

The brave girl, letting Zach know she was still there for him.

"I don't recall winning any medals in my last event," he said.

"You'll be better next time," Kate said.

"You sure?"

"Bring it," she said.

He laughed. "Right: bring it. At least one of us feels invincible. It's hard for me to even believe anything that's happened over the past few months. At times, none of it feels real."

Kate was quiet for a long minute. Then she said, "Let's take a ride out there."

They both knew where "there" was.

"You mean it?"

"I should have made you take me with you the first time," she said.

They rolled up the blanket and dropped it at the house. Kate told her mom they were going for a bike ride. Alba told them to be safe and to be home in time for dinner.

"Zach," Alba called from the kitchen. "You watch out for my girl."

"Always," he called back.

They put on their helmets, went out to Route 27 and headed east in the bike lane with Zach in the lead, occasionally yelling at Kate to pick up the pace.

"The only way for you to outrace me, Harriman, would be in a *car.*"

Maybe it was a ten-mile ride, maybe less. But the distance and time seemed to pass quickly. Once they passed through the town of Montauk, Zach remembered the route to the field as if his bike had a GPS attached to the handlebars.

When they got there, they leaned their bikes against the stone wall by the road, Zach half expecting Mr. Herbert to pop out from behind it and yell, *Surprise!*

But he didn't.

It wasn't as isolated as it had been back in November.

There was an occasional car today. A couple of guys who looked as if they were training for the local track team ran by them on the road and smiled. Zach and Kate smiled back, then hopped over the wall and headed into the field.

Five months since he'd been here.

But in a lot of ways, it felt like yesterday.

In a voice barely above a whisper, Kate said, "This feels like a cemetery."

"Maybe because it is."

New green grass had begun to grow where the nose of the plane had hit. The whole area generally looked more alive now. To Zach's eyes it seemed like less of a crater, more like a wound that had begun to heal.

Kate just stared, not saying anything.

Finally she said, "Which direction did the old man come from?"

He showed her. Then pointed to where Mr. Herbert had run away from him, into the high grass. Zach told her again how he'd followed him into that grass and ended up in Central Park, before he'd come to find her at the Knicks game.

"Wow," Kate said.

"So which is it?" he said. "Dream or nightmare?"

"Little bit of both."

They looked around in silence for a few minutes. Zach realized there wasn't much to see, really. There was just the tall grass and the sound of the wind through it and the faint crashing of ocean waves in the distance.

"You ready to head back?" he asked.

Kate nodded.

They made their way back to their bikes and strapped their helmets on. They could see the two track guys coming back from the direction of the ocean. A truck passed by.

Zach took one last look back, feeling like waving good-bye to this place. Knowing somehow in that moment he was never coming back. He'd found out as much here as he was ever going to find. If there were answers to be found, they'd have to be found elsewhere.

He reached into his pocket and felt both Morgan coins.

His and his dad's.

No heat coming off them today. No light. Nothing.

More than half a year now since his dad had died. Already he was having a hard time recalling his father's face.

"Let's hit it," Zach said, disgusted with himself.

"Whoa, nice bikes."

One of the two runners.

He was a tall redhead. His friend had a crew cut buzzed so close to his head Zach thought for a minute he'd shaved it. Both wore T-shirts with cutoff sleeves.

The one with the crew cut had a tattoo on his upper left arm that Zach couldn't make out.

He told himself they were just a couple of locals out for a run. No knit caps here. No giants.

No threat and no sweat.

"I'm sorry?" he said.

The redhead said, "I was just saying what nice bikes these are."

He turned to his buddy. "Lot nicer than we ride, right, Eric?"

In a small voice Kate said, "Zach, let's go."

The one called Eric said, "Look like they cost more than my mom's Taurus."

"Easily," the redhead said.

Eric said, "Always wanted a sweet bike like these. How many speeds you got on these babies?"

"You know something?" Zach said, keeping his voice even. "I don't even know. But if you guys will excuse us, we have to be getting back."

Eric reached out for the handlebars of Kate's bike then and said, "How about if I just take yours for a quick spin?"

Kate tried to hold on, but Eric was too strong, pulling the bike toward him. Kate stumbled as she let go, nearly falling.

"Oops," Eric said, draping a leg over the seat and sitting down.

"Give her back her bike," Zach said.

"Make me," he said.

It was on now, and they all knew it.

Zach felt a familiar heat. "Fine with me," he said.

Maybe they were just a couple of high school kids thinking they could pick on a couple of younger kids because they were bigger, because there was no one around to stop them.

They were wrong.

Somehow Zach knew the next move that was made couldn't be theirs.

So he covered the distance between him and the buzz cut with a blinding first step he hadn't used in a while and lifted Kate's bike right out from underneath him. Eric landed on the ground. He wasn't down for long, though. Zach lifted him up by his T-shirt and tossed him over the stone wall and into the field.

It should have been just Zach and the redheaded kid then.

Only, they had company.

Zach heard the truck before he saw it, turned and saw

it was the same truck they'd seen pass not two minutes ago. It had turned around and skidded to a stop on the side of the road. Two guys got out, one from the driver's side and another from the passenger's.

Coming to help?

The driver walked toward Zach and the redhead saying, "There a problem here?"

Something didn't feel right. Zach's senses were on fire. He shifted his eyes and saw the passenger about to reach for Kate.

"Zach!" she said.

Zach turned his head to her, just long enough for the redhead to get behind him and put him in a bear hug.

Worthless. Zach flipped him with ease into the driver of the truck, the force of the collision taking them both down.

And just like that, Zach knew he was *back*.

By now the other guy from the truck had Kate by the arm and was dragging her toward the truck. She kicked him, hard, in the only place she could reach—the back of his right knee. He yelped in pain and Kate prepared for another attack, but Zach beat her to it. He covered the distance between them in the air, like a gust of wind had picked him up and carried him.

Flying again.

He pulled the guy off Kate, dragged him away from

her and pinned him up against the side of the truck, hard.

"Go!" he said to Kate. "Get on the bike and go!"

She shook her head. "I'm not going anywhere," she said. And Zach knew she meant business.

The other three were all back on their feet and coming after him. No time to argue with Kate. He had to focus on them.

Zach felt someone's hand on him, grabbing for his shoulder, trying to pull him off the guy he had pinned to the truck. And it was suddenly as if Zach were everywhere at once. Elevating, spinning in the air, backhanding all of them, one after another, watching them all go down. He landed, fists in front of him, ready to spring.

One by one they got back to their feet, slowly, all of them ready to make another run.

Zach stole a quick look at Kate, who didn't look scared now or even surprised, who just stared at him and mouthed these words:

Bring it.

They spread out around him, moving in slowly. The driver of the truck was now holding a tire iron. He swung it at Zach, who slipped the shot with ease.

Keep moving, he told himself, remembering the giant.

No clean shots.

Then he rolled away from a wild punch thrown by Eric, spinning away and simultaneously kicking the legs out from underneath the redhead.

The passenger from the truck was the last one standing.

Zach looked at him.

"Bring it," he said.

Then he heard a voice behind him.

"*Stop!*"

A voice he knew, even if he'd never heard it this loud.

The old man.

The passenger seemed to shrug. "Whatever you say," he told Mr. Herbert.

Zach turned to the old man.

"They're with *you?*" he said.

"They've all been with me, Zacman. From the start."

NONE of the four hesitated. The two older men hopped into the front of the truck while the two high schoolers got into the back.

Zach and Kate just watched.

It had all been so real to them just a moment before. Now it turned out to be like they had all been actors in a scene, with Mr. Herbert the director who'd just yelled "Cut!"

"Go," Mr. Herbert said to the driver of the truck, in the same tone of voice you'd use to tell a dog to sit. He waved dismissively with the back of his hand.

The engine turned over, and Zach and Kate watched as the truck quickly disappeared, well over the speed limit, toward Montauk.

Toward the real world, Zach thought.

Kate spoke up before Zach.

"You *staged* all this?" she said. "For what—your own sick amusement?"

"It *was* a bit of a show," Mr. Herbert said, "I'll grant you that. But not in the way you think."

"And what *are* we supposed to think?" Zach said, voice rising. "You put us both in danger, or at least let us *think* we were in danger. Was the giant with you, too? You're crazy, you know that? You're a twisted, crazy old fool!"

Mr. Herbert smiled.

"You're angry," he said.

"You noticed?" Zach said. "Yeah. I'm good and ripped."

"*Good,*" Mr. Herbert said. "Use it. You're much better when you're mad than when you're moping around feeling sorry for yourself."

One more time, Zach looked down at clenched fists. His whole body feeling pretty much like a clenched fist.

"Maybe the one I should bounce around is *you,*" he said.

"We both know you're not going to do that. I'm on your side."

"Right. You're such a good friend that you ordered the

beating that sent me to the hospital. I guess you forgot to mention that the last time."

"I told him not to hold back," Mr. Herbert said. "It was an important lesson and you know it. Trust me."

Zach remembered the words on his computer screen. *Trust no one.*

"I don't," Zach said. "Trust you. My dad used to always tell me even about my favorite athletes: believe everything they do and nothing they say. That's pretty much where I am with you."

"Get over it."

He didn't sound like somebody trying to be a kindly old wizard now. Not somebody trying to be Zach's friend or a friend of the family.

Zach stood his ground. "You don't get to tell me what to do."

"I do and I don't."

"Riddles again?"

"I'm trying to help you."

"By trying to hurt me?"

The old man nodded, smiling again. "You've passed every test thus far."

"Not with the giant."

"Not at first. But it turns out you passed a different kind of test with him. Because you came back from that, boy. Like a fighter getting knocked down and getting back up. When you had to respond today, you did. Like a champion."

Kate said, "You make it sound like he's supposed to thank you."

Mr. Herbert turned to her. "Doesn't matter to me if he does or doesn't. I'm not here to please him. I'm here to make sure he's ready."

Kate started to say something else, but Zach put a hand on her arm, stopping her.

He said to Mr. Herbert, "*That's* what this has been about? Some kind of training camp?"

"I couldn't tell you that before. You had to think it was real," the old man said. "I needed to know if you're ready."

"You keep saying that. Ready for what?"

"To stand and fight."

"I'm a kid," Zach said.

"No," Mr. Herbert said. "You're a hero."

"My dad was the hero," Zach said.

"And now it's your turn," the old man said.

Now it's your turn.

The words echoed in Zach's ears. Kate was silent next to him. He didn't blame her. What was there to say to a statement like that? What did it really mean?

"Let's take a walk," Mr. Herbert said.

"I'm not going anywhere with you," Zach said. Then he looked at Kate. *"We're* not going anywhere with you. Anything else you can say, you can say to both of us and you can say it now. Or we're leaving."

"And go where, boy? Where does somebody go to escape his destiny?"

"You know my destiny, too? The way you know me and my family, even though we don't know you? And that's why you gave me these powers?"

The old man looked genuinely curious, as if Zach had finally stumped him. "You think *I* did this to you?" he said. "You're still not getting this, are you?"

He went over and sat down on the stone wall, took off his cap, ran a hand through the white hair.

"I did nothing of the kind," he said. "I couldn't."

Zach looked stunned.

"Then who did this to me?"

Kate reached over, took Zach's hand and said in a low voice, "He has a right to know."

"You're right," Mr. Herbert said to her. "He does."

"So tell us," Zach said.

"The ones who killed your father are the ones who really gave you these powers," he said. "The people you think of as the Bads."

"That's crazy," Zach said.

"I know it may seem crazy to you," Mr. Herbert said.

"And there's no way to fully explain what's in store for you. You're going to have to learn as you go. That's what I'm trying to teach you. The Bads, they don't give up, don't stop coming. *Ever.* You can never let down your guard, never get sloppy. Look at your father. One time. That's all it took. Now they're going to want you. Not dead—at least not yet. They're going to want you on *their* side." He grinned. "Like you're their prodigal son."

Kate squeezed Zach's hand. He made no move to take it away. "So Dad gave me these powers . . . not the Bads."

"Strictly speaking, yes," Mr. Herbert said. "But it was the Bads that forced the transition. One thing has never changed, across all the years and all the battles: there can only be one hero at a time."

"You make it sound like a long time," Zach said.

"Forever," the old man said, staring at him now. "That's how long the fight has been going on." He sighed. "Your dad, he always thought he'd be able to prepare you when the time came."

"Prepare me?"

"For his powers becoming your powers when his time was up," Mr. Herbert said. The old man closed his eyes. "He thought he had time, all the time in the world. He didn't. None of us do."

He shrugged then, turned and looked at the field

where the plane had crashed. "They finally took him down. And now that he's out of the way, they're coming, boy. And they're going to come hard, the way they always have when they see an opening."

"How?" Zach said.

"That's the thing," the old man said. "We don't know. We never know. But when it does come, it's going to be big and it's going to be evil, and innocent people who get in the way are going to get hurt. Or killed."

Zach said, "You make it sound like the devil himself is coming."

"And he knows who you are," Mr. Herbert said. "It's why I've been trying to give you the preparation your father didn't. Because the devil's coming for *you* this time, Zach. You're either with him or against him." He put his cap back on and stood up.

"Next time," he said, "the giants will be real."

YOU'VE had enough for one day," Mr. Herbert said. "You'll see me again, and soon."

Zach said, "How do I know you're telling me the truth about all this?"

"Because on some things you have to go on faith, boy."

"I've been warned not to trust anybody."

The old man grinned. "Good!" he said. "That means you're learning. There is one person, though, you'd better learn to trust."

"Who's that?" Zach asked.

"You," Mr. Herbert answered.

He gave a little bow to Kate, turned and disappeared into the high grass, the way he had the first time. The last thing they heard was the sound of him whistling.

This time Zach let him go.

"You think he's really on your side?" Kate said.

"I think he's on his own side," Zach said.

"Is that enough for you?"

"It's going to have to be for now."

Then he added, "But only for now."

He started walking his bike back to the road. Kate followed him with hers. They both heard the car coming at the same time, saw the headlights cutting through a dusk that had snuck up on them, the way the whole day had.

They froze as the car closed on them, slowing slightly.

It passed them and kept going.

They're coming, boy, the old man had said.

"Here's all I *really* know for now," Zach said. "That old man, crazy or not, is the best chance I've got to find out who killed my dad."

"Sounds like he knows already," Kate said.

"I think he knows the team," Zach said. "Not the player."

"What makes you so sure?"

"I don't know," Zach said. "I just have a feeling about this."

"So now what?" Kate said.

Zach threw his leg over the seat of his bike.

"The devil he talked about?" he said. "I want to see his face. I want to know his name."

THE afternoon Zach, Kate and Alba came back from Long Island, Zach's mom was waiting for them in the living room.

Along with Uncle John.

Zach's mom gave him a long hug, telling him how much she'd missed him, and when he was finally able to pull back, he looked over her shoulder and said to Uncle John, "You don't call, you don't write."

"You got me," Uncle John said. "But in my defense, I *have* been a little busy, Zachary."

Then he grinned and said, "I also thought my personal bodyguard needed a little time to heal. And to think without a bunch of voices messing with his head. Are you really doing good?"

"I am," Zach said. "We had a good week out at the house."

"Just the three of you?" Uncle John said.

He made it sound like a casual question, but his eyes didn't leave Zach for a second. Almost as if he knew something.

But how could he?

Zach answered the question without really answering it. "Quiet out there, just the way I like it," he said. "Kate and I had the beaches to ourselves."

"I'm jealous."

"So where have you been?" Zach asked.

"Lots of places, here and abroad," he said. "Hong Kong led to India, and then L.A. All of it business. All of it boring. But I'm back now to my real job, helping look out for you."

A weird answer, Zach thought. Couldn't *anything* be straightforward these days?

"Are you staying for dinner?" Zach said.

"Actually I'm taking your mom out to a new restaurant, as soon as we get some business out of the way."

"More boring stuff?"

"Senator Kerrigan's rally in the park," his mom answered.

"Our grand savior," Uncle John added with just enough sarcasm.

"Okay, that's my cue to leave," Zach said, then told Uncle John to make sure and knock on his door before they left.

He went upstairs to his room and pulled his laptop out of his backpack. No messages this time when he powered it up.

He still didn't know whether Mr. Herbert had left the last one. Or if somehow Uncle John had hacked into his computer from parts unknown, as a way of warning him about unseen dangers.

Or crazy old men.

Zach didn't know if that was possible. Didn't know who, or what, to believe anymore. He stared at his screen saver, a shot of the court at Madison Square Garden right before the start of a Knicks game, thinking that every time he got what seemed like answers, he really did end up with more questions.

Starting with this one:

If he did believe Mr. Herbert's version of things, where did that leave him with Uncle John?

Uncle John popped his head into Zach's room about an hour later, while Zach's mom was off changing for dinner.

"Hey," Zach said.

"Hey, yourself." Uncle John took a look around. "You

know, all the times I'm at the apartment, I hardly spend any time at all up here in Zach World."

"We need to talk," Zach said.

"I know."

"There's an expression guys have, when they put out a fist and have to wait too long," Zach said. "Don't leave a brother hangin'. You left me hangin' that night in the hospital."

"Couldn't be helped."

"Whatever," Zach said. "You're here now. And I think you owe me some answers."

Uncle John sighed. "This isn't the time."

"I saw Mr. Herbert again. A few days ago."

Uncle John turned around, closed Zach's door, checking to make sure it was shut. Then sat down on the bed. "Tell me all about it."

Zach did.

When he finished, Uncle John shook his head. "Same old game for him."

"*What* game?"

"He's the mischief maker, Zachary. The *trouble*maker. I tried to explain this to you that night in the hospital. Acting as if he's on your side, as if he's the only person in the world you can trust."

"He can be pretty convincing. Especially that stuff about evil coming."

Uncle John wasn't looking at Zach's computer. Even if he had been, he probably wouldn't have realized that Zach had been video chatting with Kate in her room, something they did sometimes for fun, even though they were in the same apartment.

He left it on so Kate could listen.

"Con artists usually *are* convincing," Uncle John said. "It's why they're so good at what they do. And why they last."

"He made it sound as if some very bad people are going to come after me, the same people who killed Dad."

Uncle John motioned for Zach to join him out on the terrace.

"Nobody can hear us," Zach said.

Except for Kate, he thought.

"I just want to make sure your mother doesn't," Uncle John said. "Your dad managed to keep her out of his real business all the years they were together. Now we're going to do the same. It's for her own protection."

There was nothing Zach could say to that, so they went outside, Zach leaving the terrace door open a crack, hoping Kate could still listen in. The night air was cool, and the city looked as spectacular as it always did.

"You said you know all about Dad's secret missions,"

Zach began. "But Mr. Herbert made it sound as if *he* and Dad worked together."

Uncle John said, "Did you tell him about our conversation at the hospital?"

"No."

"Good work, Zachary. The less he knows about what *I* know, the better."

"What does he want from me?"

"He wants to get close to you," Uncle John said. "But please remember, he's the one who put you in the hospital."

"So everything he's telling me is a lie?"

"No." Uncle John put an arm around him, pulled him closer. "The best liars always know how to use the truth to make their lies seem more real."

Zach looked up at him.

"What about all the bad stuff he says is about to happen?"

"That's the thing, Zachary," he said. "There's always bad stuff about to happen. He just wants to scare you as a way of making you think you need him. But he's the one who needs you, so you don't try to stop him. He's trying to trick you into trusting him by making it appear like he's some kind of wise man. It's all about trust for now."

That again.

Uncle John said, "He tried to do the same thing with your father when he was young. When he realized the scope of your father's powers. But the older your father got, the more he saw through him. Saw he was being used."

Zach heard his mom's voice, looked through the terrace doors and saw her standing in the doorway to his bedroom, pointing at her watch, more for Uncle John's benefit than his own. She said she would be waiting downstairs.

Uncle John smiled at her, put his arms up in surrender. In a low voice he said to Zach, "I think your father realized too late just how dangerous your Mr. Herbert was."

"You really think the old man is that dangerous?"

"And so should you." Uncle John leaned close as he opened the doors. "The one who's coming after you is him," he said. "The evil is already here."

ONE of them is lying to you," Kate said.

"Brilliant deduction," he said. "Do you want to be Sherlock Holmes or the other guy?"

Kate had heard everything. Now they were going over all of it, like spreading the pieces of a big puzzle out on a table, trying to match parts together.

"Mr. Herbert is so convincing," Zach said.

"So is your Uncle John," Kate answered. "By the time he finished, he had me scared that I'd even been around that old man."

"But if the old man is the one who's telling the truth," Zach said, "if he's one of the good guys . . ."

Kate looked sideways at him. "It means your Uncle John isn't."

Now that was on the table, too.

"What do I do?" he said.

Kate said, "You're not going to like what I'm about to tell you."

They were out walking again, on East Broadway, heading toward the East Side. A light rain began falling.

Zach waited.

"You're going to have to treat your Uncle John like a suspect for the time being," she said.

"I can't!" he said.

"You have to," Kate said. "They're each giving you a different version, but for now, Uncle John is the only one around."

Zach said, "I feel guilty even having this conversation. Even talking about not trusting him."

"It's not like it's a ton of fun for me, either. Don't forget, I've grown up with him, too."

"He's Uncle *John*," Zach said. "Not only was he my dad's best friend, now he's my *mom's* best friend."

"But what if *he's* the one who's the mischief maker?" Kate said. "I know you don't want to think about this—but what if the evil has been right in front of you your whole life?"

Zach had no answer for that. And Kate was right: he didn't want to think about that. So he put up his hand and said he'd spring for the cab fare home.

"My hero," Kate said.

He sure didn't feel like one today.

Another night lying in the dark in bed, staring at the ceiling, laptop finally turned off, everybody else in the apartment asleep. Zach unable to.

Again.

He thought about all the trips his dad had taken over the years. Had they all been top-secret missions? Had they all been about capturing Bads, about good conquering evil? If so, did it matter who Tom Harriman had really worked for—the president or the old man?

Zach's mission was different and hadn't changed from the moment he'd decided that his dad's death had not been an accident. He was trying to catch bad guys, too. The bad guys who'd killed his dad.

And no matter how confused he felt sometimes, no matter how many times he got turned around, Zach knew he was getting closer.

Either Uncle John or Mr. Herbert was lying to him, that much was certain. Both were doing whatever they could to win his trust and discredit the other. One of them knew a lot more about his dad's death than he was saying . . . maybe even both.

Zach couldn't think about it any longer. He needed to move, needed to get out. He could feel the anger rising up in him at two-fifteen in the morning, surrounded by the silence in the apartment.

He put on a gray hoodie, jeans and sneakers. Went through the kitchen, flying down the back stairs in a way he never had before, but a way that felt perfectly natural now—going from landing to landing, feeling as light as air. When he got to the lobby, he peeked out and saw the front door open as Ziggy, one of the night doormen, went outside for a smoke. Zach was through the lobby and through the door, invisible until he was two blocks up, out of Ziggy's sight.

Fresh, he thought.

The old man had said Zach was better when he was angry, had told him to use his anger, and tonight he was going to use it to blow around the city. A different kind of knock-around day, at a new speed.

The speed of me.

He headed over to the West Side, down to Greenwich Village, and then all the way downtown to the Financial District. Wall Street, the old buildings regal and gleaming against the darkness. The hole in the ground, filled for now with iron girders and construction cranes, that used to be the Twin Towers, another scorched piece of earth caused by the Bads. Then up to 42nd Street, all the way to the top of the Chrysler Building, the entire city

visible beneath like some high-def video game. Shouting at the top of his lungs at invisible opponents, telling
them to come out and fight.

He didn't know what time it was or where he was
going next, he just knew that this feeling wouldn't leave
him, that he wasn't nearly ready to go back home.

No sleep tonight.

When he was tired of being up above the city, he went
underneath it, rode the Lexington Avenue subway back
downtown and then right back uptown, passing through
Grand Central on the return trip, knowing he had to
think about getting home. It was five o'clock by now, and
he didn't want to be sneaking back into his room as Alba
was getting up.

He got out of the subway and came up the steps outside the 68th Street station.

"You lost, little dude?" he heard a voice say.

It belonged to a guy at the top of the steps. Black
T-shirt, black jeans, spiky hair. A young guy, his eyes
looking a little unfocused, like he was on his way home
from some club, like he might be a little spaced out.

He looked almost as jittery as Zach felt.

Zach ignored him, took the last two steps in a little
hop. The guy stepped in front of him, smiling.

One more test? Zach wondered.

One more game organized by the old man?

Was the old man watching from somewhere, wanting to see how Zach would handle this?

Or was this threat real?

Zach didn't care.

He grabbed the guy before he knew what was happening, lifted him off the ground, had him backed up into an alley before the guy could say another word.

"Hey!" he said. "Hey, relax, dude, I was just messin' with you."

Eyes focused just fine now. On Zach's.

Clearly scared by what they saw.

Zach said, "What's the matter? You don't want to talk anymore?"

He bounced him hard against the side of the building.

"Come on," Zach said. "Let's talk. Ask me another question."

"Let me go, man. Please. Let me go."

The air came out of Zach then, like the whole night coming out of him, hearing the guy beg to be let go.

Zach released him, the guy afraid to move at first, not sure what Zach was going to do. Then he ran out of the alley, disappearing toward Third Avenue, giving one last look over his shoulder.

Zach unclenched his fists, put his own back against the brick wall and slowly slid down it.

When his breathing was back to normal, he stood up, still not sure how he'd stopped himself from giving the guy a beating, *why* he'd stopped himself. Just glad that he had. Maybe it was hearing something in the guy's voice he used to hear from kids at school when guys like Spence would bully them.

In that moment, Zach saw more than he had all night, even from the top of the Chrysler Building. He recognized the dark side of what he could do now. Of what he'd become.

No matter how much he'd scared the guy, Zach Harriman had scared himself more.

IN sports, they talked about shutting players down when they got hurt.

Shutting them down for a game or two, or even for the rest of the season.

Zach shut himself down after that night outside the subway. He wondered if his dad's powers had ever scared him like this, if he'd ever had to fight to keep the dark side of himself under control. Zach had never imagined his dad having anything close to a dark side. He was too good for that. *Wasn't he?*

But maybe I'm not, he thought.

Maybe I'm not worthy of these powers.

Not because of what he did to that guy by the subway. Because of what he'd *wanted* to do to him. What he was *capable* of doing now. Now not only was Zach afraid of trusting Mr. Herbert and Uncle John . . . he was afraid of trusting himself.

Trust no one, the message had said.

Was it right?

What if Mr. Herbert had been telling the truth about the trouble headed Zach's way? Didn't he need to be prepared just in case?

He hadn't told Kate what happened that night, because he was ashamed of the way he'd acted and what he'd felt. He didn't like the Zach in the alley, and he was pretty sure Kate wouldn't like him, either.

So he kept getting up and going to school and trying to act normal, wondering what was going to happen next.

And when he would figure out who to trust.

He missed his dad now more than ever.

It was a Wednesday afternoon and Kate had a student council meeting after school, so Zach decided to take his reading homework with him to Central Park.

It was one of those days in the place his mom called "the dream New York." No clouds in the sky. Temperature around seventy degrees. The park alive with colors. He had just a few more of Hemingway's short stories to read, his teacher having told the class to save the best until last, one called "A Clean, Well-Lighted Place."

So he took his book to one of his favorite corners of the park, close to the apartment, a rock formation in the trees above Conservatory Pond. It was one more thing he knew about the park that he wasn't sure how many New Yorkers did—how much water was scattered throughout the place.

Eight hundred and forty-three acres in all in Central Park, and this place up in the rocks was one of his favorites, beautiful and peaceful and quiet. Nothing like the other places that had become battlegrounds for him, with Spence and Knit Cap and the giant.

He opened up his book and was alone with Hemingway, trying to make sense of what the man in the story was really talking about.

"Hello, kid."

Somehow Zach wasn't surprised or even startled to see Mr. Herbert sitting there next to him on the rock.

"Miss me?" the old man said.

"Actually, I did," Zach said. "But it's not as if I can call you on your cell or text you. Where *do* you live, by the way? Or do you just hang upside down at night?"

"I move around," the old man said. "I make it my business to be hard to find and harder to reach. It's safer for me that way."

"Whatever," Zach said, promising himself he wasn't going to let the old man get under his skin today, no matter how exasperated he got.

The old man leaned back, letting his face take the sun. "Nice spot," he said.

Zach said, "My Uncle John calls you the mischief maker."

He decided not to waste time today, to put Uncle John right in the old man's face and see how he reacted. His dad always used to tell him that you didn't want to be the guy who joined the debate, you wanted to be the guy who set it.

Mr. Herbert laughed. "Probably said a lot worse about me than that, knowing John Marshall."

"As a matter of fact, he did."

"He and I have never seen eye to eye, about your dad or anything else. From the beginning, we just seemed to rub each other the wrong way."

"He also said that I don't have to wait for the bad stuff that's coming my way; he said it's already here."

"How's that?"

"He says it's you."

The old man laughed again. "Just trying to scare you, kid. Was a time when I had my own powers. Real powers. Now I'm just a shell of what I used to be. No, your Uncle John's just trying to keep you out of the line of fire. He was always trying to get your dad to quit, especially at the end. He thought the world had gotten too dangerous for him. And that he'd lost a step. Not physically. Mentally, he meant. It wasn't easy having to be him."

"But my dad wouldn't quit."

"No," the old man said, "he certainly would not."

There was a part of Zach that wanted to just get up and leave, get away from this old man who'd already caused him so much grief, who'd said he'd purposely tested him, all in the name of helping him be his father's son.

It sounded ridiculous.

But if they hadn't been tests . . . then what? That giant could have done a lot more than just put Zach in the hospital with some busted ribs if he'd wanted to. And who really knew how hard Knit Cap and his friends had been trying?

Zach knew that if Mr. Herbert wanted to cause him real harm, he could have done it a long time ago.

So he stayed right where he was.

"You don't hate Uncle John the way he does you?" he said.

"I don't hate people just because I disagree with them," Mr. Herbert said.

"I listen to you," Zach said, "and then I listen to him and have no idea what I'm supposed to be doing."

"I explained this already, boy. You just need to be

ready. Because if there's a way to stop them when the time comes, you're going to be right in the thick of it."

"How can you know some disaster is coming and not know what kind? Or where?"

"Who said I didn't know where?"

"Here we go again," Zach said.

The old man put up a hand. "Hear me out," he said. "Did you know what or where that morning you followed Kate?"

Zach thought a second. "No," he said. "I just had a feeling."

Mr. Herbert nodded. "My point," he said. "Sometimes you know without really knowing. Sometimes we know just enough to get the jump on the bad guys."

He winked at Zach.

"Sometimes we sit around waiting for something that takes a long time arriving. If we don't, or if we're wrong, then the Bads win the battle. Bridges get blown up. Buildings topple." He sighed and in that moment looked older than ever to Zach. "Planes crash. People die. But we keep fighting."

People die.

Like all those people in the Twin Towers.

Like Zach's dad.

"You're still the best chance I have to find out who killed my dad," Zach said. "And I *am* gonna find out."

"But even if you don't, you still gotta keep fighting."

There was the sound of sirens in the distance.

Zach said, "So why did you drop in on me this time?"

"I have some new information," the old man said. "When it does happen, it's going to be in New York."

"Here?" Zach said.

"Here," Mr. Herbert said. "C'mon. It's time for class to begin."

"What," Zach said, "now you're my teacher?"

The old man winked at him again.

"Think of me as Yoda," he said, "just with an edge."

They spent the next hour looking for secluded areas of the park, something that wasn't so easy to do on a beautiful day.

"Tell me again why we're doing this?" Zach said.

"Because you still don't know how good you are," the old man said. "Or bad."

Zach thought about the guy outside the subway station, wondering if the old man knew about him.

"What does that mean?" Zach asked.

"You're both, Zacman. And you've got to *use* both, just the way your father did. It's part of the deal."

They found an empty spot in the woods behind a statue of a sled dog named Balto. They worked on the East Green, a huge lawn up near 72nd Street and Fifth.

At one point, Mr. Herbert disappeared into the woods near the Navy Terrace, which overlooked another one of Central Park's ponds.

"Where are you going?" Zach said.

"You'll find me."

"I haven't played hide-and-seek in a long time," Zach said.

"Imagine your friend Kate needs you," the old man said. "Imagine that up good."

Zach closed his eyes and remembered that morning Kate went by herself to the park. He felt something inside him focus.

He opened his eyes. Zach was able to look across the water and into the woods and spot Mr. Herbert immediately, like he had x-ray vision.

When the old man came back, he said to Zach, "Next time it might not be a game."

They practiced a few more times, Zach acing every test. It got to the point where Zach could hone in on Mr. Herbert from anywhere. Once he figured out how to do it, how to focus his energy, it was almost too easy.

Finally, they ended up near Bethesda Fountain, another rock formation.

"Are we done?" Zach asked.

Mr. Herbert said, "For today."

"Good," Zach said, and stretched out on his back, suddenly exhausted by everything.

But he was excited, too; he couldn't help it.

He was smiling.

"What's good?" the old man said.

"Just thinking of something one of my friends said at school today."

It was a lie. Maybe Mr. Herbert knew. If he did, Zach didn't care.

He was smiling because something Mr. Herbert had said before turned out to be right on the money, not that Zach would ever admit that to him:

Zach *hadn't* known how good he was.

Not even close.

The old man stared at Zach as though he could see right through him. Then he, too, smiled.

"You may just be ready, Zacman."

THE rally for Senator Kerrigan was scheduled for the last weekend in June, in the famous section of Central Park between 79th and 85th known as the Great Lawn.

Zach's mom told him she had been a teenager when the singing team of Simon and Garfunkel had given a free outdoor concert on the Great Lawn. She and her girlfriends had gone and felt as if most of the city went with them that night.

"They said it was half a million people in the crowd," Elizabeth Harriman said.

"To see two guys sing?"

"It was a big deal at the time because it was a reunion concert."

"New York makes everything bigger," Zach said.

"Paul Simon has agreed to sing before Senator Kerrigan speaks in June," his mom said. "It's that big of a deal."

"You think he can help you pull half a mil this time?" Zach said.

"Oh, Lord no," she said. "But we think there might be a couple hundred thousand. That's how much momentum the campaign has picked up over the last month."

Zach high-fived her. "That's my mom right there, ladies and gentlemen, talking about the big 'Mo.'"

"C'mon, you know it's happening," she said. "I'll bet kids are talking about the campaign in your school."

"Actually, they are," Zach said. "Most kids think Senator Kerrigan is cool. And the political geeks who are really following it talk about Vice President Boras like he's Darth Vader."

"Good," his mom said. "It's nice to hear they totally get it at the Parker School."

Zach was a week from the end of school, two more finals to go. But he'd done his studying before he came home today, so now in the early evening they were waiting for Uncle John to come over for dinner, the first time he'd been to the apartment in a few weeks. As usual, he'd been traveling.

And for the first time in his life, Zach had been glad about Uncle John's absence. There was something between them now, some barrier, whether it belonged or not.

Tonight, though, was different, from the time Uncle John stepped out of the elevator. Tonight it was as if he was determined to be the old Uncle John, being funny about all the candidates in the campaign, smiling through the dining table debates with Zach's mom about Senator Kerrigan and Dick Boras, maintaining that Boras was better qualified to be president.

"Maybe you should go work for the man," Zach's mom said.

"And risk the wrath of Elizabeth Townsend Harriman?" Uncle John said. "I am stubborn, madam, but not stupid."

"I was watching you when Bob Kerrigan spoke here," she said. "You were as engaged by him as anybody else in the room."

Zach was sitting next to Uncle John, who poked him lightly with an elbow now and winked. "Nobody fakes sincerity better than I do," he said.

"Except Dick Boras," she said. "The man's a menace."

"No, he's a realist," Uncle John said. "Of all the candidates, he's the one who truly understands best how dangerous the world has become, even better than his boss in the White House. Not just a dangerous world, but fragile at the same time." He looked at Zach and said, "It's like a ball game, where you're always one play away from winning or losing."

Zach's mom hung with him. "You're saying Bob Kerrigan is somehow *oblivious* to how dangerous things are?"

"Dick Boras wants to win for the good of this country. That's not enough for Bob Kerrigan. He's more concerned that people like him. He's *desperate* for it. Dick Boras doesn't care if you like him or not. He doesn't particularly care if you love America. He just wants things to work better. He gets things *done*."

"Are you saying he wants to get the trains to run on time?" she said. "Isn't that how dictators used to sell themselves?"

Uncle John laughed, waved his napkin like a white flag. "I give up," he said. "I'm the lawyer, but every time we have this conversation, I feel as if I'm the one on trial."

"And at least you're not being an old crab about things this time," Zach's mom said.

"At least I'm consistent," he said. "You know I used to have this same argument with your husband all the time."

Zach didn't know if Uncle John knew about his dad being Senator Kerrigan's running mate, even though he acted like he knew everything. But Zach wasn't about to bring it up.

Zach's mom asked Uncle John if he had time for coffee and he said no, it was such a nice night he was actually hoping he and Zach could go for a walk.

"I've been an absentee uncle way too much lately," he said. He looked at Zach and said, "So, you up for it? Could be some kind of mondo banana split at the end of it."

"Yeah, man."

Zach's mom said fine with her, she had some calls to make anyway. Uncle John promised he wouldn't keep Zach too long. Then Elizabeth Harriman kissed them both on the cheek and she was gone.

It was in the elevator when Uncle John turned to Zach and said, "This isn't about going for ice cream."

"Didn't think it was."

"We need to talk," Uncle John said.

They walked up Fifth when they got outside. Once they were out of earshot of the doorman, Uncle John got right to it.

"I don't know what kind of nonsense the old man has been feeding you about picking up where your father left off," he said. "But you're not ready to do that."

"How do you know that the old man has been feeding me anything?" Zach said.

"It's my business to know things," Uncle John said, "whether you want me to know them or not."

"You never told me I was supposed to let you know every time Mr. Herbert dropped in on me," Zach said.

"And you, young Zachary, should have enough common sense not to have to be told." He put his hand on Zach's shoulder and gave a gentle squeeze.

"Maybe I would share more things with you if you weren't so hard to find."

"I'm not mad at you," Uncle John said.

"Same," Zach said.

"It doesn't change the reason we're having this talk," Uncle John said. "You're *not* ready."

"For what?" Zach said.

"You're too smart to play dumb with me, Zachary. You know what I'm talking about. You're not close to being ready to be the kind of game changer your father was. Someday, yes. But not now."

"Mr. Herbert says the two of you have never agreed on anything. Him and you, I mean."

"Finally," Uncle John said, "we agree on something."

They had taken a right turn, were walking the short block toward Madison.

"But *you* made it sound like more than just a dis-
agreement, Uncle John. You said he was the enemy."

"In my world, Zachary, the enemy is anybody I don't
trust. Your father always trusted 'Mr. Herbert'." He air-
quoted the name with his fingers. "I, on the other hand,
never did. He always said he was on your father's side. I
never believed that for a second. I frankly always thought
his endgame was trying to convince your father to work
for the other side."

"For the Bads?"

"Yes. For the Bads." He put quotes with his fingers
around "Bads."

"You both make them sound like some kind of army,"
Zach said.

"And wouldn't be wrong," Uncle John said.

"Do they have some top-secret headquarters?" Zach
asked.

Now they were walking south on Lexington. But
somehow this didn't feel like aimless wandering to Zach,
a knock-around night.

They were going somewhere with this.

"You mean, where are they?" Uncle John said. "They're
everywhere. Everywhere in the world that there's trouble. Or an opening. Everywhere they think they can
get an edge, from sea pirates to the Middle East. Every-

where they think they can replace a good leader with one of their own. Or put weapons into the wrong hands." He shook his head, annoyed. "Everywhere where they can make their mischief. Only it's not simple mischief. Most of the time it's life and death. And there have been too many times when the old man has been in the middle of it. I don't believe in coincidences, Zachary. And neither should you."

"Do they . . . do the Bads have guys who can do what I do? What my dad did? Do *they* have game changers?"

He was asking as many questions as he could, not sure when he'd get another chance like this.

"Probably," Uncle John said. "I don't know for sure. I can only speak for our side. And even though it sounds like some fable, something that should involve a sword in a stone, on our side there's only ever been one hero at a time." The same thing Mr. Herbert had said.

"How long has this been going on?"

Uncle John looked at him. "For a *very* long time."

"And now it's my turn."

"*Eventually* it's your turn," Uncle John said. "*Not* now. Perhaps I should have told you these things before, but I'm telling you now because I care about you. And I want to protect you."

"Mr. Herbert says I'm ready now."

"Mr. Herbert doesn't know you like I do!" Just like

that, Uncle John, who almost never raised his voice, was shouting. "All he's ever been interested in is helping himself! But this time I'm not going to let him. I won't allow him to put you in harm's way. I wasn't able to save your father. I can't even *think* about what would happen to your mother if anything happened to you."

They kept walking in silence down Lex, past delis, hip-hop sneaker stores, fruit stands and bars. On the next corner was a new Carvel. Uncle John asked if Zach wanted to get an ice cream after all. Zach said no.

They hooked a right, headed back toward Fifth Avenue.

Zach said, "What if Mr. Herbert is right, and something terrible is about to happen, and I might be able to help stop it?"

"Zachary . . . ," Uncle John said.

"I'm just sayin'."

"Haven't you been listening? You *still* won't be ready," Uncle John said. "There will be dragons for you to slay someday, Zachary. Just not now. Just because you have the physical weapons doesn't mean you're ready to use them. There are consequences. And for what it's worth? I think he's making the whole thing up. I told you that night in the hospital not to believe a word he said and I'm telling you again now."

Uncle John turned, put his hand on Zach's shoulder

again and said, "This isn't your fight. Not yet, anyway. Take some time and enjoy being a kid. You're fourteen, for cripes' sake."

Zach had one more question.

"There's something I need to know, Uncle John. It's been bothering me for a while. I've never asked Mr. Herbert, but I'm asking you: if my dad was an orphan, who passed on his powers to him?"

"Your father always wanted to know that, too," John Marshall said. "Who his real father was. He used to say that even Superman knew who his father was. But not Tom Harriman." He pointed a finger at Zach and said, "But I always felt the old man knew, even if he swore he didn't."

"How could he?" Zach said.

"Because I believe he and his people killed him."

HE *said* that?" Kate said.

"Sure did," Zach said.

"Uncle John told you that Mr. Herbert is the one responsible for your dad being an orphan? But didn't you tell me that Mr. Herbert *found* your dad when he *was* an orphan?"

"Welcome to my world," Zach said.

"Wow."

"Uncle John said that he didn't have any proof, but that he never believed my dad had just been left at the hospital as an infant, which is what he'd always been told. He believed that if Dad had these powers, then so did *his* father. And that only someone who wanted control of the next generation would have killed the father to get to the son."

"Like some kind of royal succession or something."

"Yeah," Zach said. "Like that."

"What he's really saying is that Mr. Herbert did to your grandfather what somebody did to your dad."

"Nice, huh?"

They were in Kate's room, Kate sitting cross-legged on her bed, Zach sunk into the beanbag chair on the floor. Both eating popcorn.

"So how do you find out if he's right?" Kate said. "Uncle John, I mean?"

"Well," Zach said, "it's not like the next time the old man pops in on me, I go, 'By the way, I've been meaning to ask you, what did you do to my real grandparents?'"

Kate smiled. "You don't think he'd make a full confession at that point?"

"I asked Uncle John if he ever shared his theory with my dad. He said he did—once. And that he and my dad had gotten into the biggest argument they'd ever had in all the years they'd been friends. He said my dad refused to hear anything bad about the old man. My dad obviously trusted Mr. Herbert. But Uncle John said it was that trust that killed him."

"So what now?" Kate asked.

"I have a plan," Zach said.

. . .

Senator Kerrigan's speech in the park was a week away, and had completely hijacked life in the apartment.

Along with Zach's mom.

Even Zach and Kate had gotten swept up in the anticipation, both of them volunteering to make phone calls to potential voters, urging them to attend the rally and send a message to the rest of the country.

It had been Kate's suggestion for them to join the effort. She thought it might be good for these calls to come from young voices, since there would be so many teenagers who would be voting for the first time in the November election.

"You're hired!" Elizabeth Harriman had said that night at dinner. "Both of you."

"Feels more like I'm being drafted," Zach had said. Then he'd pointed to Kate and said, "She *likes* talking on the phone."

"C'mon, you stiff, it'll be fun," Kate had said.

And then his mom had reminded Zach that he'd be doing his part to help elect somebody in whom his father had believed so strongly.

"Oh, nice, Mom. Play the Dad card." Because enough time had passed that they could joke about his dad sometimes.

"Who knows," his mom had said, "maybe someday

you'll want to go into politics yourself. If you do, you can tell people about how your first campaign was for a friend of your father's."

It was late June, and school was out by then. So each morning Zach and Kate would get their lists and set themselves up in the dining room, which had been turned into a Kerrigan war room. Then for a couple of hours they'd make calls on the senator's behalf from opposite ends of the long dining room table, wearing the cool headsets Zach's mom had provided.

When somebody would say to either Zach or Kate that they sounded pretty young, they had a scripted response, and a good one.

"Old enough to care about America," they'd say. "And about our future."

Then in the afternoon, Zach would go to the park and wait for Mr. Herbert to show up again.

Zach had asked him after their day in the park, "How can I find you if I need to reach you?" Mr. Herbert had said, "If you really need me, I'll know, Zacman. And I'll find you."

Zach had been with the guy exactly four times in his whole life, twice at the crash site, once in the hospital, once in the park. Still, he felt as if the guy was somehow *running* his life, as he kept running Zach in circles. With

Uncle John telling him to run the other way. It was crazy, so much of it seeming unreal.

Yet there was no denying it: his powers were real.

Like his sixth sense for things.

It had been kicking in more and more lately, without warning. Not something he could summon, not some kind of crystal ball he could use to gaze into the future.

Just part of who he was now, what he could do.

Zach had first started noticing it at school—little stuff, like knowing when a pop quiz was coming. The week before, his mom had come home a day early from a trip to the Midwest, wanting to surprise him. Only he hadn't been surprised. He'd known walking home from Parker that she'd be waiting for him in front of the building.

Maybe, he thought, this was something that had started the day his dad had died. That feeling he had sprinting across the park that day. Knowing something was wrong, just not knowing what. Or knowing how bad it really was.

Maybe it was this same sense, this same feeling, that kept drawing him back to Central Park.

So he was back in the park today, on the rocks above Conservatory Pond, suddenly sure the old man would show up.

"Zacman."

No sound of footsteps, no warning. Mr. Herbert, sitting next to him as if he'd been sitting there all along, staring out at the water the way Zach was.

"Did you train my father here?" Zach asked.

"Among other places."

"Uncle John says that Dad trusted you."

A sad look crossed the old man's face, taking Zach by surprise.

"Not completely," Mr. Herbert said. "Never completely."

He gave his head a quick shake, then gave Zach a light whack on his back and said, "Something else is on your mind. Spill."

Zach wasn't surprised. "You told me that something bad is going to happen in New York. Do you think it could have something to do with Senator Kerrigan?"

Mr. Herbert smiled. "Using that sixth sense, are you?"

"I guess so," Zach said. "But his speech would obviously make a good target, with so many people in one place."

"And with the senator such an influential person these days . . . ," said Mr. Herbert. "*So* influential, in fact, that it makes a person wonder . . ."

"What do you mean?" Zach shot back. "Wonder about what?"

"I'm just saying," Mr. Herbert answered. "It's like that line from *Spider-Man,* 'With great power comes great responsibility.' It's true."

"That would have made it true for my dad, then."

"And now for you," Mr. Herbert said.

"Do you have any reason to distrust Senator Kerrigan?" Zach asked.

"I have reason to distrust most people," he said. "But I'm not the one the good senator has to worry about, am I? Like I told you earlier, the Bads are always looking for an opening. Evil is smart, boy. Never forget that."

Zach was certain he wouldn't.

THEY decided to train for a couple of hours. Zach found himself doing things he had never imagined. Like catching small rocks thrown by Mr. Herbert as though the old man had turned into a pitcher with a hundred-mile-per-hour fastball. Like following the flight of a bird from tree to tree, half a mile away. Finally, the old man stood, nodded and turned to leave without a word.

"Wait," Zach said.

Mr. Herbert stopped, turned slowly back toward Zach.

"What you said the other day . . . you really think I'm ready?"

"Seems to me you'd better be," Mr. Herbert said.

He tipped his baseball cap to Zach, a small gesture,

the way baseball pitchers do to the crowd when they are taken out of a game. Then he walked off.

Zach walked toward Fifth Avenue, occasionally looking over his shoulder, watching the old man walk across the Great Lawn in the direction of Central Park West, toward the West Side buildings that framed that side of Central Park.

Then he followed him.

It was easy.

Zach never worried about letting him get too far in front of him, having *totally* sharpened his long-range vision the way Mr. Herbert had taught him, knowing that if he had to, his eyes could track the old man all the way to the Hudson River. When he concentrated, it was as if everything peripheral melted away, all the cars, buildings and people.

He couldn't believe he hadn't tried this before, tried to find out where Mr. Herbert went and who he talked to, where he lived.

Who he really was.

Maybe I am *learning,* Zach thought.

The old man walked south on Central Park West, taking his sweet time, as if enjoying the early summer afternoon. And Zach was sure that even if he had turned around, he would never have noticed the kid in the long-sleeved Knicks T-shirt a hundred yards behind, because that was another one of the things Mr. Herbert had taught him, how to be a blur when he wanted to and not just when he had to, making himself disappear as he went from one place to another.

Making himself invisible.

Mr. Herbert walked past the Museum of Natural History on 81st Street, Zach wondering if *he'd* ever gone inside to check out the dinosaurs. Or maybe they didn't hold any fascination for him. Maybe he was as old as they were.

The old man headed west from there, walked over to Broadway, stopped inside a Starbucks, came out a couple of minutes later with a cup of something hot, sipping gingerly as he walked.

Then he turned downtown, walking all the way to 72nd Street—a wide, loud, busy street with traffic going in both directions. From there Mr. Herbert headed east, walking back toward the park now.

Zach wondered if they were just going to keep circling this way for the rest of the afternoon. But then Mr. Herbert stopped before crossing Central Park West, stopping right in front of the Dakota, which Zach knew was a New York City landmark. John Lennon had lived there and was shot to death just inside the gates. The building towered over this corner of the West Side like some elegant old castle.

Mr. Herbert pulled out an old-fashioned pocket watch, approached the doorman and spoke to him briefly. The doorman went inside a little booth, made a quick call from inside, then came back out. One set of iron gates opened, then another set behind them, and the old man walked through.

Zach could have made it across 72nd and through the gates before they closed if he'd wanted to.

But he didn't.

He knew why the old man was here.

And it wasn't to see where John Lennon had been shot.

He was here to see another John who had lived here for as long as Zach could remember:

Uncle John.

ZACH stood on the south side of 72nd, staring at the gates of the Dakota, where the shooter had been waiting for John Lennon that night. Uncle John had shown him the spot one day.

Zach briefly tried to talk himself out of any conspiracy theories. There were a lot of people who lived in that building, right? Just because Uncle John lived at the Dakota didn't make it automatic that Mr. Herbert was here to see him.

But he was.

Zach's sixth sense told him so.

All along he had listened to both of them, smart enough to know that *some* of what he was being told had to be the truth. What was harder to figure out was *which* parts.

And which were lies? Now he wondered if the bits and pieces that both of them had been feeding him had been their way of playing a kid, and that all of it was one gigantic lie.

But why?

If Uncle John and Mr. Herbert are on the same side, what do they want from me?

Why had they spent so much time trying to pull him in opposite directions?

Zach was on his own.

And it was time to stand up for himself.

He would wait for Mr. Herbert as long as it took.

There was a pizza place halfway up the block. He went inside and ordered a slice and a Coke. He came back out, polished both off, leaned against a wall. And waited.

An hour later, Mr. Herbert emerged through the gates. Zach was across 72nd in a flash, not worrying about traffic, moving so fast that traffic didn't have to worry about him.

"You were here to see him, weren't you?"

He expected Mr. Herbert to at least be a little bit surprised. But he wasn't.

"You followed me," he said, with a nod.

Not a question.

"Good boy," he added. "The *invisible* boy."

"I'm not looking for a pat on the head," Zach said. "What were you doing in there?"

"I was trying to help you," he said.

"You know what?" Zach said. "Sometimes I think I've gotten just about all the help from you I need. Or want."

"You don't understand," Mr. Herbert said.

"Try me."

The old man made a gesture behind him that took in the Dakota. "He doesn't know what's best for you," he said. "He never understood what was best for your father, couldn't get his mind around your father's true destiny. It's time he learned. It's time he let go."

"Uncle John says that you only do what's best for *you*."

He nodded.

"Used those same words just now, as a matter of fact."

"And do you?"

Mr. Herbert didn't blink. "Used to, perhaps. Maybe I still do. Who's to say?"

Zach felt heat rising to his face. He couldn't hold back.

"Tell me why you're here!" Zach said. *"Tell me what you want!"*

In a quiet voice, with that sad face on him again, the old man said, "Because I want to make things right."

Then he was across the street in a flash. Across the street and into the park.

Gone.

Nothing to follow this time except a trail of words. The old man invisible himself.

ZACH bolted across the street and into the park, thinking: *It won't be so easy to lose me this time.*

He was wrong.

Powers or no powers, he'd lost the old man. Again.

And he'd left Zach with one more riddle to solve:

What had he meant by making things right?

Zach thought about going back to the Dakota, telling the doorman that John Marshall had another visitor. But he didn't think he'd get the truth out of Uncle John, either. He'd just spin things his way again, play Zach a little more, try to make Mr. Herbert out to be the bad guy.

Zach felt angrier than ever.

Not angry at the old man or Uncle John. No, now he was angry at the man he'd always trusted more than anybody.

His dad.

For not preparing him.

For not telling him what was coming.

For dying.

Zach felt the same kind of rage coming up within him now that he'd felt that first time at school, with Spence Warren, the day he'd tried to knock down a brick wall with his bare hands.

"You're angry?" Mr. Herbert had said one time. "Good. Use it."

But how did he use this kind of anger against his dad? How did he take a swing at somebody who wasn't even there?

When he was almost to Fifth Avenue, about a block from the apartment, Zach stopped. Looked down at fists that were clenched again.

Opened them.

And saw that each was holding one of the Morgan coins.

His and his dad's.

Zach stood there looking at them, palms up. *Staring* at them. Almost as if he was waiting for them to do something, to be some kind of coin trick all by themselves. Waiting to feel the heat come off them. Waiting for the light.

Nothing.

Just like the one his dad had been carrying when his plane went down had done nothing for *him*.

Good *luck* charms?

Where was the luck?

He closed one fist now, then the other. Then he turned and threw the coin in his right hand as far as he could into the park.

Then he threw the other one.

There was nothing magical or lucky about them.

Now they were like his father.

Gone.

Zach dropped to the ground right where he was.

And for the first time since his dad died, he cried.

IT was the night before the big rally.

Zach and Kate had gone over to the park in the afternoon with Zach's mom as she made what seemed like her tenth trip for what she always swore were her "final" preparations.

They listened to Paul Simon's rehearsal, Zach still trying to imagine what the Great Lawn was going to look like when it was filled with two hundred thousand people.

Or more.

Two hours later they were back at the apartment, Zach's mom still at the park.

They were searching his dad's office.

"Tell me again why we're doing this," Kate said.

"Looking for clues," Zach said. "Some heads-up he might have left me without actually knowing it would be a heads-up."

"Like what?"

"We'll know when we find it," Zach said.

"It feels creepy," Kate said.

"I know," Zach said. "And I know about being creeped out."

He told her about the day he'd been alone in the apartment and came upstairs to find the message on the laptop: *Trust no one.*

Kate was at one of the bookshelves built against the wall. She turned now, her face serious.

"What is it?" Zach said.

"That was me," she said.

Zach was in the chair behind his dad's desk.

"What?" he asked.

"I said it was me."

"No, it wasn't," Zach said.

"Was."

"You weren't even there! It was one of the reasons I freaked at the time. The apartment was so empty and quiet except for me."

Kate said, "You think you're the only one who can sneak in and out of here? The only difference between the two of us is that I don't need superpowers to do it."

It was as quiet in there now as it had been that afternoon.

"But why?" Zach said.

"I finally got sick of you being like the rope in a tug-of-war between that crazy old man and your crazy Uncle John. So I thought I'd do something to get your attention."

"You never told me you don't like Uncle John," Zach said.

"Let's just say I never loved the guy," Kate said. "Too slick. Always listening to everybody else's conversation even when he's supposed to be talking to you. Too charming. I kept my mouth shut about it because I know you love him." She looked at him now with big eyes. "Or did," she said. "And after what happened to your dad . . ."

"So why didn't you just say something?"

"You wouldn't have listened."

"I always listen to you."

She smiled. "You listen. But you don't always hear."

"So that was your way of trying to scare me straight?"

"Maybe a little bit. There was so much drama and

mystery and freakiness going on—*still* going on—I thought leaving you a secret message was the best way to get your attention."

"Well, guess what? It worked."

"*Yes!*"

"You want to hear something nuts?"

"Please don't say you suspected it was me all along."

"No," he said. "I thought it might be . . . might somehow be my dad. I thought, just for a second, that he was still looking out for me."

"Oh, Zach," she said, "I never meant for that to happen."

"I know," he said. "I thought it was one more thing that couldn't be explained in a normal world, or what used to be a normal world. And that he had found a way to send me a message."

"You know something? I actually believe your dad would have given you the same message I did."

Zach nodded. He reached into his pocket and felt the now-familiar emptiness. No coins to feel solid in his hands. Nothing to tell him all would be all right.

Help me, Zach thought. *Dad, I don't know how to deal with all this.*

That's when his eyes landed on the framed cartoon strip his dad had always kept by the side of his desk. It was an old strip called *Pogo*. Pogo is sitting in a swamp and the caption reads:

"Yep, son.

We have met the enemy.

And he is us."

THE house phone chirped just as Zach finished getting dressed for the rally—his mom having been dressed for hours—and Alba told them Senator Kerrigan was on his way up.

The plan, Zach knew, had always been for him to stop here, then for Zach and his mom and Kate to get in one of the cars in the motorcade taking them all into the heart of Central Park.

"I still don't understand why we just can't walk over," Zach said.

"Because," his mom said, "this isn't one of those days when Central Park is the personal playground of Zach Harriman."

It turned out the senator even had two Secret Service guys with him for the elevator ride up to the apartment.

The Secret Service men stood guard as Senator Kerrigan hugged Zach's mom, then turned and told Kate how pretty she looked in her summer dress. When the senator turned away, Zach couldn't resist pointing to his own cheek, his way of telling Kate she was blushing.

She shot him a mean look back.

Then the senator came over and offered Zach a low five. "Hear you've been working the phones for me," he said.

"No big deal," Zach said. "I felt like I ought to do something more than just watch the whole thing from the sidelines."

"I'll take all the help from the Harrimans I can get," the senator said.

He leaned down a little so he and Zach were eye to eye.

"We would have made a great team, your dad and me," he said. "This is going to be his campaign as much as it is mine, you can trust me on that."

Then he said to Zach, "My aides make fun of me, because I say this all the time, but this is going to be the best day of the campaign yet!"

All along, Zach had wanted this to be that kind of day for his mom, because of all the work she'd done, because this was the first thing that seemed to make her really happy, her old self, since Zach's dad had died.

But he *did* want it to be great for Senator Kerrigan, too, maybe because the senator reminded him of his dad more and more.

Maybe heroes still *could* win the day.

The rally was scheduled to begin at one o'clock.

Senator Kerrigan had told them he'd been over to the Great Lawn yesterday, practicing his speech in front of policemen and Secret Service men and workers still making the finishing touches on the stage, and the invisible bulletproof shield that would run the length of it.

"A *shield?*" Zach said.

"Not my style, believe me," the senator said. "It's the world we live in, son."

Zach understood more than he wanted to.

When they all went downstairs at noon, Zach saw that Fifth Avenue had been shut down in both directions. There were three limousines waiting, one for the senator and a couple of his staffers, another for more of his staff and one for Zach and his mom and Kate. All around the limousines were police cars with flashing lights and more policemen on motorcycles. Photographers and television cameramen were behind both sides of blue barricades on the sidewalks, with still more police keeping them back.

When everybody was ready, they pulled away from the building.

"Wayyyyyy cool," Kate said, sinking back into the plush seat of their stretch.

"Still think we should have walked it," Zach said.

"Poo on you," Kate said.

"Good one," he said. "Poo. You *are* smarter than a fifth grader!"

She punched him.

The limos pulled up next to the huge tent that had been erected behind the stage. When they got out, Zach saw more blue barricades and rope lines, police everywhere and more Secret Service in dark suits. On either side of the Great Lawn were two temporary stands for television cameras and photographers.

"Why so much protection?" Zach said to his mom.

"Because the people in charge of doing the protecting *hate* wide-open spaces like this."

Paul Simon was inside the tent, guitar slung over his shoulder, a Yankee cap on his head, chatting with the senator. Zach's mom went off and seemed to be talking to everybody at once, as if these were the last moments before the biggest party she was ever going to throw in her life.

Zach and Kate had been given the kind of all-access passes to wear around their necks that they gave you at concerts. They walked out of the tent and around to the side of the stage.

It was then that they got their first good look at the crowd on the Great Lawn, and it was more than he had imagined, more people in one place than Zach had ever seen in his life.

"O . . . M . . . G," Kate said.

"Tell me you just didn't say that," Zach said.

But the truth was he felt the same way.

It looked like a concert audience, with some people sitting on blankets, others standing and dancing to the beat of the music blaring through the loudspeakers. And for all the security in the area, what Zach really saw were happy faces, more young than old, waiting to hear the senator's speech.

Like it *was* a party.

"Tell me you're not crazy excited," Kate said.

"I am," he said, and before he knew it, the mayor was introducing Paul Simon and this huge roar exploded from the crowd as he began to sing "Mrs. Robinson."

Zach couldn't help himself now, his senses were in total overdrive, like the energy of the day was trying to short-circuit them. He *was* excited, too excited.

The way he became when his sixth sense knew something was about to happen.

IT is my high honor to welcome to our great city the next president of the United States . . . Senator Robert Kerrigan!" The crowd was cheering so wildly by the end of the sentence that even with a microphone, the mayor's words could hardly be heard.

Zach's heart was beating faster now, and not just because the big moment had finally arrived.

All his senses, new and old, were telling him that something was *very* wrong.

It was as if all the noise had dropped away, the cheering, the applause, all of it.

Zach felt as if he were alone in the park all over again.

He heard a voice inside his head then, clear as day. His father's voice. Telling him:

Look.

Then again:

Look!

"At what?" he said.

"What?" Kate said.

But Zach wasn't talking or listening to her. He wasn't even scanning the crowd with Secret Service eyes. His eyes had stopped roaming. They were trained on the skyline, the grand skyline on Fifth Avenue.

Again he heard his father's voice.

"Look to the sky, Zacman."

Zach Harriman did.

It was there, outlined against the sky, on the roof of a building, that he saw a shooter where a cop in riot gear had been before.

Zach's eyes closed on him now, the guy crouched between two ancient turrets up there.

Zach focused not just on the black outfit he was wearing, the black ski mask, but his finger on the trigger of his rifle.

The angle was perfect, off to the side and just high enough to take the shield out of play, to give the guy a clear shot.

The gun taking dead aim at the man who'd just been introduced as the next president of the United States.

THE shooter's hand seemed as clear and sharp as if he were holding it up in front of Zach's face.

Senator Kerrigan was trying to quiet the crowd, holding up his hand and saying, "Thank you. Thank you so much. My fellow New Yorkers. My fellow Americans."

Zach heard none of it.

Just saw the sniper pulling the trigger.

No time for Zach Harriman to shout out a warning, no time to get the attention of the Secret Service. No way for him to be heard over the roar of the day.

Only time to fly.

Out of nowhere Zach was just *there*, driving his shoulder into Senator Kerrigan the way Spence had once done to him, knocking him away from the podium, sending him to the ground as the bullet intended for him blew a hole through the Kerrigan for America sign behind him.

Everything had happened at once after that. Secret Service men covered the stage, guns out, Zach using strength that must have surprised Senator Kerrigan, yelling, "Stay down!" at him loud enough to be heard over the screams from the crowd on the Great Lawn.

Another shot fired.

Then Zach was the one being blindsided.

He was sent flying to the stage, facedown, as a voice next to his ear screamed:

"Down, Zacman!"

The old man.

Out of nowhere again.

The old man's arms were around him, pinning him down. "Always gotta watch out for the second bullet, boy."

The two of them were surrounded by Secret Service and pulled away from the senator. Another group of Secret Service surrounded the senator, half pulling, half dragging him off the stage.

The crowd was frantic, screaming, trying to leave the area. Police shouted into blow horns, telling everyone to please remain down.

Zach noticed none of it. He had only one voice in his head. His own.

Thank you, Dad, the voice was saying.

Thank you.

They were safely back in the tent now. Zach, his mom and Kate were seated at one of the tables, his mom still shaking from the assassination attempt, asking Zach every fifteen seconds or so if he was really all right.

"I'm fine, Mom. Really," Zach said.

"I still don't understand who that old man is," Zach's mom said. "Or where he came from."

Zach wondered where to begin, how exactly to explain. Fortunately, he was spared when his mom's cell phone rang. She yanked it out of her pocket and smiled when she looked at her caller ID. She said, "Unknown caller indeed." Then she answered it, nodded and said, "He's right here."

She handed Zach the phone. "Somebody wants to talk to you."

Zach took the phone and said, "Hey."

"Zach, it's Bob Kerrigan. I want to thank you for saving my life."

Not knowing what else to say, Zach said, "You're welcome. Sir."

"The Secret Service got the shooter. We're all safe for now, thanks to you."

Zach wondered just how safe that was.

The senator said, "I'm going to be a little busy the rest of the day, but I plan to stop by later and thank you in person. And maybe you can explain to me how the heck you did what you did."

"I did what anybody would have done," Zach said.

"No, son, it isn't what anybody would have done," the senator said. "Your father, maybe. And you. But not anybody."

He said good-bye and Zach handed the phone back to his mom. "Let's go home," she said.

"In a minute, Mom."

He was looking past her now, to where Mr. Herbert was about to slip through an opening in the tent as though no one could see him.

"I've got to thank somebody, too," Zach said.

For the second time, Zach followed Mr. Herbert. The old man moved slowly, heading for a small cluster of trees behind the Great Lawn. He eased himself down to sit at the base of a tree, seemingly inch by inch until he could no longer stop the momentum and he dropped the remaining distance. He closed his eyes. He looked older to Zach than ever. Ancient.

And tired.

Zach closed the remaining distance and stood over him. Mr. Herbert, his eyes still closed, smiled. "Took you long enough," he said.

It was then that Zach noticed the blood on the old man's hands. And the widening circle of red beneath the leather jacket he always wore.

"You're hurt!" Zach said. "Let me call somebody!"

He started to turn, but the old man held a firm hand on his leg.

"Like I told you," he said. "Always watch out for the second bullet." He swallowed, his breath sounding heavy. "Turned out this one had my name on it."

"You need a doctor," Zach said. "Let me go get my mom, she's got her phone."

The old man put a finger to his lips.

"Hush, boy," he said, then patted the ground next to him, motioning for Zach to sit.

"Let me die in peace," he said. "With my grandson next to me."

YOUR—your grandson? . . ." Zach knew he was stammering.

The old man hadn't moved, his right hand resting on his knee, his left hand clutching his stomach.

"Hush," he said again. "And listen."

Zach started to say something, but the old man held up his hand, shaking, as if it took all the strength he had left.

"Your father died before his time," he said. "I thought I could save him, too, went halfway around the world trying. But they tricked me into thinking it was *that* plane, the one with him and Vlad the Bad on it. Once it landed in London, I thought he was safe. But it was the plane after that. His." He coughed, a bad sound. "The one taking him home."

He began coughing harder, as if there was no way for him to stop.

This is crazy, Zach thought. *My grandfather. I can't lose someone else.*

The old man peered into Zach's eyes and seemed to read his mind.

"Don't worry, boy. I long ago outlived my time. Lived a lot longer than I deserve."

"But my dad . . . my dad was an orphan."

"In a way he was. That's what everyone needed to think. It was the only way I could keep him safe. If they'd ever known I had a son, they would have used that against me. Or taken him. Even later, when he was older, they never knew he was mine. Maybe because he had real character to go with his powers. They couldn't turn him as easily as they'd turned me when I was young."

Zach felt like he was falling.

"Your father was my one true thing," the old man said. "The one who was going to do enough good to make up for all the bad I did. It's why I couldn't let them near him."

"One hero at a time, that's what my Uncle John told me," Zach said.

"Yes, Zacman, he was at least right about that, there's been a long line of us. A long line of heroes. At least until I came along. The black sheep of the family. The one who only cared about being wanted for his powers. The one who thought he could play both sides. Which made me no better than the dark side in the end."

"The mischief maker."

"Your Uncle John never knew *who* I was. But he knew *what* I was."

"And Dad never knew?"

He shook his head and that triggered another coughing fit, the weak sound of it piercing Zach's heart. Time was growing short. "No, he never knew what a bum his old man was. I watched over him from a distance at first as Tom went from group home to group home. But your father couldn't be held in one spot, as though, even then, he knew the world needed him. Myself, I was getting into too much trouble. I knew my time as a hero was about to end, so I took in my only son. I never told him who I was. But I told him about the magic. I showed him his destiny, just as mine was stripped away. It was too late for me." He took in a labored breath. "For your father, it was only the beginning. Just like it is for you. The secret's out now, boy. You won't be able to hide from it. The Bads will try to turn you to their side. If you turn them down, they'll try to kill you. It's that simple. Be true to your heart, boy. Being on the side of good can mean a lonely life. But not as lonely as giving in."

"My dad," Zach said. "He would have wanted to know. If I were him, I would have wanted to know."

In a voice Zach had to lean closer to hear, the old man said, "He would have been ashamed."

He grabbed Zach's shirt and pulled him closer. In a whisper, he said, "But never of you, Zacman. Your father would have been proud today."

His fingers released Zach's shirt.

"Very proud," he said with a smile.

Then his eyes closed one last time. For good.

ZACH slipped past the security guard and the doorman like a gust of wind. He entered the elevator and pressed the button for the fifth floor, just like all the other times in his life he'd come here.

Except it wasn't like all the other times.

"Zachary!" Uncle John said with a big smile when he opened the door. "The hero of the day!"

"That's me," Zach said.

He walked into a living room that had always felt as much like home as his own.

"I owe you an apology," Uncle John said. "You were more than ready for today, weren't you?"

"He's dead," Zach said.

Uncle John's face turned serious. "Who's dead?"

"Mr. Herbert."

Uncle John glanced out the window, then back at Zach. "I'm sorry," he said.

"Are you?" Zach asked. "Really?"

Uncle John inhaled deeply, then let out the breath slowly.

"No," he said. "The crazy old man had it coming."

"How can you say that?"

"Zachary, you're much better off without him. I tried telling you once already—this isn't your fight."

And that's when Zach knew for sure.

The last time he ever saw his dad, that evening he went to the movies with Kate. When he'd been too busy to watch the Knicks game with his dad. He'd walked in on the tail end of a phone conversation. His dad's words that evening echoed now in his head. "The ones who tell you not to fight are the ones you should fear the most."

"It was you," Zach said.

"What was me?"

"On the phone that night with my dad. The night before he left and never came back. It was you telling him to stay home and not to fight."

Uncle John sighed.

"Yes. I wanted him safe."

"Did you?" Zach said. "Aren't you the guy who told me

that the best liars use the truth to make their lies more real?"

There was that roar inside Zach now, one he was starting to know all too well. So much running through him. He gave his head a shake, trying to quiet his brain, knowing he had to focus.

"No," he said.

"No . . . what, Zachary?"

"No, you didn't want him safe. No one knew my dad like you. No one. You said so. You knew he'd ignore your advice. You wanted him to."

Uncle John reached out a hand. "Zachary . . ."

"Stop! You may not have been the one who brought down his plane. But you as good as murdered him yourself. Same as you allowed those shots to be fired today."

Nothing. No denial this time, or even an attempt. Just dead, empty eyes, no longer able to meet Zach's.

"You *allowed* my dad to be killed. Why?"

Uncle John's face was tight as he answered. "Because he stopped listening, that's why. Not just to me . . . to anyone. He thought he knew it all, could do it all himself. Then he decided the role of a hero was no longer enough. He had to have more. The White House. Sure, it was just vice president for now. But after? What then? Your dad wanted to run this country."

"So what?" Zach said. "He would have been a great president."

"A president is a leader, Zachary. Your father was a one-man show. A man who was rapidly making a lot of enemies. You can't act like that and expect to become leader of the free world."

"So you stood by and let them kill him."

Uncle John paused a beat. Now he was the one who looked ancient, tired. "You don't understand," he said. Then: "This was larger than me. Larger than one man."

Zach looked out the window. Looked at Central Park, the trees and grass that for years had felt like his own backyard. Now everything felt foreign, cold.

"And what about today?" Zach said. "What about Senator Kerrigan?"

"I had nothing to do with that," Uncle John said. "You have to believe me."

Zach didn't.

"I'm so sorry it had to end that way," Uncle John said. "You have to know I mean that."

"What I know is that you're scum," Zach said. "Don't talk to me, ever again, don't come near me, don't come near my mother."

"You can't afford to be that way, Zachary. The whole world knows about you now. You need me more than ever.

The Bads will be coming. They're going to try to turn you into one of them."

"The way they did you?" Zach shot back.

No denials there, either.

"You've got to listen to me, Zachary. Really listen. There's a lot you don't know about this world yet."

"I know one thing," Zach said. "I finally know what the devil looks like. He's the one you trust and then betrays you."

"You don't know what you're up against. The bullets today? They were nothing. They were just the beginning. I know these people. You don't know what power they have. The way you can't even begin to know the powers you're going to have."

Zach heard Kate's voice in his head. It made him smile.

"Bring it," he said.

"What?"

"I said, 'bring it.'"

Then Zach Harriman turned and walked out. Through the door, down the elevator, across Central Park West and into the park. Feeling something new inside. A calm strength. A confidence. This was his life now.

And he was ready.

Zach began to run. Not flying this time, just running.

Pumping his arms and legs and running into the heart of the park, toward whatever lay ahead.

Zach Harriman was home. Not worried about watching his back now. Just thinking that the Bads better watch theirs. He wasn't worried about them chasing him, not anymore.

From now on, he was chasing them.

COCHRAN PUBLIC LIBRARY
174 BURKE STREET
STOCKBRIDGE, GA 30281